"Honey"
The Continuing Adventures
of a Young Cowboy

Stu Campbell

This is a work of fiction and the second book in A Young Cowboy's Adventure series.

ISBN: 978-0-9675164-8-6

Edited by Mira Perrizo
Cover and text design by D.K. Luraas
Cover painting by Larry Jones, Bouse, Arizona
Author photo by Elizabeth Dobbs

Printed in the United States of America

Contents

Other Books by Stu Campbell

The Letter

When we got home, Mom was fixing supper and asked, "What did you get?"

"Just some pants an' shirts," I replied.

"Let's see," she said.

"You're busy with supper," I said.

"There's nothing here that can't wait while I look at your new clothes."

I was to find out that women can always take time out to look at and discuss new clothes.

I took the clothes out of the bag and set them on the table, expecting to be chastised for my selections. I did pick the stuff I liked.

"This is a very pretty shirt," Mom said, holding up one of my selections, "but it's a ladies shirt."

My dad walked in as my mother held up the shirt.

"Are you buying your mother clothes?"

"No," I said. "It was on the clearance table, I liked it, so I bought it. It didn't cost much."

"You'll be laughed out of school when you wear that," Mom said. She had a funny grin on her face.

"How do you tell the difference? They were all on the same table," I said.

"A man's shirt buttons, or snaps in this case, from the left. A woman's shirt snaps from the right, like this." Mother demonstrated how the snaps came over from the right on the shirt.

I was beginning to think I had a lot of things to learn that they didn't teach in school.

"I'll put it in the top of my closet an' take it back next time I go to town. I got the receipt in the sack. I sure ain't goin' to wear it!"

"But it's a very pretty shirt," said Mother. "I'm sure you would look very nice in it." Mother still had that funny grin on her face.

"I don't think so," I replied adamantly.

I took the clothes to my bedroom and put them away. I put the ladies' shirt in the top of my closet, reminding myself not to wear it. I put the receipt on top of the shirt so I could exchange it the next time I went to town. Then I sat down on the bed, reached in my hip pocket and pulled out the letter.

I had carried the letter in my pocket ever since I got it and it was getting a little worn and dog-eared. I read it every chance I got, when I could read it in privacy. I was puzzled by it and didn't know what to make of it. I had given it a considerable amount of thought. I knew I should answer it, but didn't really know how or what to say.

The letter, written in a very feminine hand started out with, *"My dear Stupid, Dumb, loving Cowboy;"*

When I first read it, I was puzzled at the introduction. The words "my," "stupid," "dumb," and "cowboy" were capitalized.

The others weren't. It was as if she was trying to empathize something. It didn't occur to me all at once, but slowly it dawned on me, this was not a love letter!

I thought this girl cared for me, a little at least, but this letter was not starting out in a complementary manner. I thought I even cared for her, a little, and had even given some thought to entering some team roping contests with her in the future. She was a good roper.

My thoughts of roping with her diminished as I read and considered her introduction. She was right about one thing; I was a cowboy, and a darn good one for my age, I figured. The fact that she capitalized "cowboy" and "dumb" and "stupid" did make me wonder. She was right about the cowboy, but was she right about the dumb and stupid? Perhaps she was joking.

I wondered about this before I read on. I wanted to make sure I was reading this letter right. If she really thought I was dumb and stupid, there wouldn't be much sense in continuing to read the letter. I took a long time thinking about this and couldn't arrive at a conclusion. I decided to read on, carefully.

The letter continued,

"I got all dressed up in my best dress to say goodbye and you didn't even get off your horse to say goodbye. I was totally heartbroken. I thought when you kissed me the night before, it had meant something, but it seems like it didn't.

I had to stop here. I didn't remember kissing her, but I do remember being kissed by her. It was the first time I had kissed or been kissed by a girl, and I was thinking it had been a dismal failure at best. While it was exciting and kinda pleasant, during the ride home I had come to the conclusion that I might not attempt it in the future if I couldn't be more sure of the outcome. The fact that I didn't know what I was doing and had no idea about how to learn didn't help much.

The letter went on and said something about going back East to go to school and going shopping for new school clothes. She ended with,

> *My dad says he'd hire you next summer and he'd like to have you work for him. He's got a few colts to start, so you have a job if you want one.*
> *Love,*
> *Sally*

I read the first part of the letter over and over, and the end. It was nice to know I had a job for the following summer, although I had no idea what kind of money I would make. I was doubtful about working with Sally until I knew where she was coming from and where she was going. I really didn't know how she was thinking.

Answering the letter was kinda difficult. I didn't really know what to say and I was giving it considerable thought. I figured I would answer it while I was in school, in study hall.

The following Tuesday, school started. I was never an outstanding student; some of the subjects, like math and English were extremely difficult for me. I did like gym and psychology. History was boring, depending on the era or century that was being studied. Social studies was mostly about politics and I didn't have much interest in that.

The first week of school ended and I really missed the freedom I had experienced on my trip home. Then I was my own boss and could do as I pretty much pleased as long as I didn't lose sight of my main objective. In school, I had a timetable to follow and I didn't make it.

On Saturday, I saddled up my horse, Roman, and rode out to look at the cattle and find my old saddle horse Charlie. I had some chores to do to help my dad, but I had a few hours to be by myself and do some thinking. I was mostly thinking about what I would write to Sally. I had a pretty good idea by the time I got back and decided I would write to her during my study time at school.

I found Charlie and he looked good. My brother Tommy had used him during the summer, but he was in good shape. I rode back to the ranch house and turned Roman loose. Matilda, my burro, stayed close to the ranch with her colt Sassy. I had originally given Matilda the name Sally, but changed her name after I met the girl Sally. I thought of this as I turned Roman loose.

My sister, Betty, had taken a liking to Sassy and the little burro followed her everywhere she went around the ranch.

I spent the rest of the day and Sunday helping out on the ranch. There was always some fence to be fixed or something to be done and I got involved in that.

I was so involved in helping out on the weekend that I forgot what I was going to write to Sally. I spent most of the study hall hour in school trying to remember what I was going to write. I did make some notes, just in case I should remember.

When I got home from school, Mother said, "There's a letter for you on the kitchen table."

Without looking, I knew who it was from. I picked it up and started for my bedroom to read it.

"Be sure and change your clothes before you start outside to do your chores." Mothers have a way of reminding a boy what to do, even when they know what to do.

The letter was perfumed and the smell really became apparent when I opened it. It started out,

You Jerk,

    I thought you might at least have the common courtesy to answer my letter. I have checked the mail every day and haven't heard a word from you, even after we've offered you a job. You haven't even taken the time to apologize for your lack of manners when you left and I got dressed up for you. You had better write and let us know what your plans are for the summer before we hire someone else. You really need some help in the social graces.

    Love,
    Sally

A short note, but very direct and to the point. I didn't know whether to be happy I got it or upset at the tone. As I pondered this, Mother hollered to the bedroom, "Are you changing your clothes? You still have chores to do. I swear, lately you seem to be in a different world."

"I'm just about ready," I said. I went out and started my evening chores, resolved to answer Sally's letters the next day in study hall.

I entered study hall the next day, armed with both of Sally's letters. I started my letter very carefully.

My Dear Miss Wilson,

    I appreciate receiving your correspondence of late. I do apologize for not answering sooner, I have been very busy with school and my chores on the ranch. I didn't realize you had got

*all dressed up just to see me leave. I don't know what I would
have said had I known. I didn't know that I was Dumb and
Stupid and I surely appreciate your bringing that to my attention, however, I am trying to remedy that situation by going to
school now.*

*I do appreciate your offering me a job. I need to talk
to my dad about what plans he has for me and see what he
thinks of the idea. I don't know what the wages are and what
is expected of me, although being Dumb and Stupid, I don't
think much. You will be pleased to know that I have a class in
social studies and when we get to the part about social graces,
I will pay close attention.*

Best Always,
Your Dumb, Stupid Cowboy

With out reading my reply, I put it in an envelope, bought a
stamp in the administration office, and put the letter in with the
outgoing mail. I wasn't sure how my letter would be received,
but her letters were answered and I felt like a big weight had
been lifted off my shoulders. I was also curious to know if she
would answer it.

The evening chores seemed a little easier that night having
finally answered Sally's letters. After supper, I went to my room
saying that I had some homework to do. I took out Sally's letters, read them both again and carefully put them in my dresser
drawer for safekeeping. The first letter was becoming quite worn.

A week went by and I got another letter from Sally. I had
been somewhat concerned that I wouldn't get a response, but it
does take awhile for the mail to operate.

Once again the letter started out,

My Dear Stupid, Dumb, loving Cowboy;
I'm not sure school will help you much, unless you work
at it.

The letter went on to tell me about the classes she was taking in school and some of her school friends. I was surprised when she wrote,

Some of my girlfriends are amazed to find that I have
a boyfriend and he'll probably be coming out to the ranch to
work this summer.

I wasn't surprised to read this. Sally surely was attractive enough, I thought she wouldn't have any problem finding a boy-friend. I thought to myself, *If I wanted to have her as my girlfriend, I had some competition.*

I hadn't given much thought to a girlfriend. I did know some girls at school, but they had different interests than I did. They were just casual friends. And I was sure none of them could rope as good as Sally.

The letter continued,

You'll have to talk to my Dad about wages for the sum-
mer. However, the tips are good and we do pay a bonus at the
end of the season.
Dad does have some colts to break this year and I have a
two year old that you can start riding.

I was a little surprised to find out that the Wilson's had some colts to break. I hadn't seen any brood mare bunches while I had been at the ranch the previous summer. The prospect of starting some colts was inviting and I wanted to get some more information. I was becoming more interested in this summer position, although I had pretty much made up my mind to go to work for them before I left the ranch the previous summer.

The letter ended,

> *By the way, Stupid, social studies doesn't have anything to do with social graces, but if you find out anything, let me know.*
>
> *Love,*
> *Sally*
> *P.S. – What's with this "Best Always"?*

I knew that social studies didn't have anything to do with the social graces but included that as a joke in my letter. I was having a tough time figuring out if Sally was serious or joking or just sarcastic. I did know that I cared for the girl and if I wanted her for a girlfriend, I was going to have to do something. Just what, I didn't know. But if she already had a boyfriend, I knew I would have to be fairly affirmative.

She ended all her letters with "Love," but I thought this was just a common courtesy used in all correspondence. I really didn't know much about love and thought "Best Always" would be proper without committing myself.

School continued throughout the fall. Letters from Sally arrived every Monday. On Tuesday, I answered Sally's letters in study hall, without being too forward.

Thanksgiving was a four-day holiday from school. At the ranch, we used Friday, Saturday, and Sunday to gather cattle. There had been some snowstorms and the cattle naturally came down from the high country. We still had to ride the high country to look for stragglers and it was cold, but it was a welcome vacation from school.

The cattle were gathered and put on the hay fields close to the ranch for the winter. The calves were weaned, the steers separated from the heifers and put in the corrals to get the used to eating hay out of a feed bunk.

Dad and I went through the heifers and selected some for replacements a week after Thanksgiving. Then we went through the cows and selected some for culling. We picked a few bulls for culling, too.

"I'll have to go to a bull sale this winter to replace them," said Dad, as I closed the gate into a separate pen to hold the bulls.

"I'd sure like to go with you to the bull sale," I said. I really wanted to go to the bull sale, not so much to get out of school, but to get some education regarding this ranch business. I had decided that this was going to be my career.

"We'll see how your grades are before I make a decision regarding that," said Dad.

My schoolwork had been suffering a little due to my helping out on the ranch and my preoccupation with Sally. I wasn't a very good student to start with. I had been using my study hour at school every Tuesday to write to her.

The first few days after weaning were always noisy. Calves were bawling for their moms and a few of the cows were bawling for their calves.

But it soon got relatively quiet.

The following week, we had big semi trucks and trailers come in to haul our calves out. Dad had contracted the sale of the calves earlier in the year, as he did every year. "It's a good idea to lock in the price early to cover the possibility of a sudden drop in the prices in the fall," he reasoned.

I would counter with, "What if the price rises?"

Dad would counter with, "We still know what we'll make if the calves weigh out. And they do every year."

A week after the calves were shipped, a semi truck showed up to haul the culled cows and bulls to the sale barn. We had enough cull stock that we had to have another truck and trailer come the following week to haul what we had left.

From the numbers of cattle we had shipped, I figured we'd have a pretty good paycheck for the year. This was good right before the holidays. My dad even made the comment that Christmas might come on time this year.

We made ready to start feeding the cattle through the winter. Most years we had to start feeding around the first of January. This year would be no exception. We turned the horses and my burros out; we wouldn't need them until March when we started calving.

My sister didn't like the idea of turning Sassy out. Those two had formed quite a relationship over the last few months.

Winter

Christmas was coming. I hadn't given much thought to it and hadn't even been to town to do any Christmas shopping. I had been buying my stamps and envelopes at the administration office at school, and while I had tried to keep my correspondence with Sally a secret, the office staff at school was beginning to suspect something. I was getting some grins and outright laughs when I went in to buy my "supplies."

Dad, Tommy, Betty, and I got in the truck and went out and cut a Christmas tree. Us kids decorated it while Mother cooked supper.

One day, a package was on the kitchen table with my name on it. I was surprised. I hadn't expected anything for Christmas outside of my immediate family. And I hadn't really asked for or needed anything specific.

"What's in your package?" My mother was curious.

"I don't know," I answered, as I tore off the outer wrapping. The inside was wrapped in Christmas wrapping with a card bearing the notation, **"Do Not Open Till Christmas."**

I instinctively knew who it was from. I didn't even have to look at the return address.

"It's a Christmas present," said my mom. "Put it under the tree, you can open it on Christmas."

I had a problem. I hadn't done any Christmas shopping and hadn't even been to town since before school started. Riding the bus to and from school didn't leave any time for going into town for anything. But apparently Sally had got me a Christmas present, and I hadn't got anything for her. I thought I was making some progress through the mail with her, even though she had a boyfriend. Her letters were not as sarcastic as they had been in the beginning.

"Mom," I said after putting the present under the tree, "I need to go to town an' do some shopping."

"I don't see how that's possible," said my mother. "We've got plenty to do here and school takes up most of the day."

"But it's real important I do some shopping. I haven't got anything for anybody for Christmas! That includes both you and Dad!" I didn't want to say that I needed a present for a possible girlfriend.

"You better talk to your father about going to town. I didn't tell you, but I picked up something for you to give your father when I was in town last week."

"How much did it cost? Dad will say no, just because it's a long way into town."

"Talk to your father anyway."

At supper that night, I brought up the subject. It met with the expected response, "There's too much to do around here," said Dad. "And you can't take a day off from school for Christmas shopping, not with the end of the term tests coming, and your grades not doing too well."

"But I haven't got anything to give Mom for Christmas!" My request was starting to sound like a plea.

"I did get something for you to give your mother for Christmas when I was in town with her last week. Don't worry about it."

"What about Tommy and Betty?"

"Your mother and I also got something for you to give to them," said my dad.

"But I already had an idea of what to give them. What if I give them too much?"

"What were you going to give them? You can't give too much, you know," said Dad.

"I thought I'd give Tommy Charlie an' Betty Sassy."

"That will work," said Dad. "But a special trip to town is out of the question for you, even though your mother is going to town during the week."

I had a problem. Sally had sent me a gift for Christmas and I hadn't got her anything. The progress I thought I was making was going to be lost.

I went to my room, very dejected. I laid down on the bed trying to figure out what to do. As I looked bleakly around the room, my eyes fell to the closet. The ladies shirt I had mistakenly bought and had not returned was still there!

My problem was solved! The only thing remaining was how to get it wrapped and mailed.

"Mom!" I wasn't supposed to yell in the house, but I had got caught up in the excitement of the moment, having solved a serious problem. "Can I have some wrapping paper and some tape?"

I started to run out of my room.

"Don't yell in the house, son. Yes, you can have some paper and the like. But what do you have to wrap and who are you giving it to?"

"It's that ladies shirt I bought by mistake an' never took back. I can send it to Sally for Christmas." I had let it slip and I had tried to keep it a secret, although Mother had surely seen the name on the return address on all the letters. She hadn't said anything though. But I had let it slip.

Mother asked, innocently, "Who's Sally?" She handed me the wrapping paper and tape. "Do you need a box to send it in?"

"Nope. She's a friend I met last summer," I said, as I took the paper and tape from her. I started to turn back to my room to wrap the shirt.

"Is Sally the girl whose been sending you all the letters? It seems like there has been one a week."

"Yes," I said.

"Do you want some help wrapping that shirt?"

I thought about it. My wrapping skills weren't too great. "It might be a good idea to have some professional help," I said.

"I think I have a box upstairs that might work well for that shirt. You go get the shirt and I'll get the box."

It seemed like hours before Mother returned with the box. I had the shirt on the kitchen table, waiting for Mom when she returned.

"That sure is a pretty shirt," she said, as she rolled out the Christmas paper. She handed me the sales receipt. "You don't need this. Will this shirt fit her?"

"It should," I said. "She's not any bigger than me."

"Tell me about your young lady friend," said Mother, curiously.

"There's not much to tell," I said. "She can ride a horse and she's a real good roper. Her dad owns that dude ranch I worked on for a spell last summer."

"How old is she?"

"She's my age," I said.

"What color is her hair?"

"Blonde."

"What color are her eyes?"

Mother seemed to be asking a lot of questions and taking her time wrapping the shirt. In an effort to get her to hurry wrapping the shirt, and to get her to stop asking questions, I answered, "One's blue an' the other's brown."

"What?" My answer and apparent attempt at humor had shocked my mother.

"They're both blue. Do you think she'll like the shirt?"

"It's a very pretty shirt," answered Mother. "She should like it very much. I'm surprised you did your Christmas shopping way back in the beginning of September, before school even started. You were really thinking ahead. What did you get me, way back in September?"

"I wasn't thinking of Christmas when I got this shirt. It was a mistake; I didn't know the difference between men's an' women's shirts. As far as what I got you, you'll have to ask Dad."

"Tell me more about this Sally," said Mom.

"I don't know what to tell you."

"Is she pretty?"

"I think so."

"Do you have a picture of her?"

"No."

"What has all your correspondence been about?"

"Mostly just girl stuff," I said. "She writes a lot about school and what her friends are doing. She asks me what school is like out here and I answer her questions. I think she's got a boyfriend back there an' havin' a present to send her might help me out some."

I didn't tell Mother that Sally thought I was stupid and dumb and a jerk. I thought that was kinda personal and I wasn't sure if Sally was just being sarcastic.

"Now we need something to wrap the present in to send through the mail. Get some of those old grocery bags and we'll wrap the present in them." Mother knew all the little tricks.

"You had better address this, or it won't get where you want it to go. Use the laundry marker."

I addressed the package from memory. I knew the address by heart, having sent a letter once a week. With the package addressed, I ask Mother, "What did I get Dad for Christmas?"

"You'll see," she replied.

"What does this young lady think of you?" Mother was not giving up on questioning me.

"I'm not sure," I answered. "She's got a boyfriend, so I don't know where I stand. But I think it was nice to get a present from her."

"You might want to send a note along with this package."

"Yes, but what would I say?"

"You could tell her you received her package and you can't wait to open it," said Mother.

How did she know I couldn't wait to open the package? Perhaps she had noticed how I looked at it every time I passed the Christmas tree. But Mom was good at knowing just what to say. It occurred to me that I should have asked for her help in knowing what to write to Sally. However, if Mom were to help me answer the letters, she'd have to read them. I resolved to get some help from her in the future, if I could, without letting her read the letters.

"When do you expect to see her again?" Mom jolted me back to reality.

"Probably this summer. Her dad offered me a job for the summer an' I need to figure out what to do."

"Does your father know about this job?"

"I haven't talked to him about it yet," I said.

"I can probably smooth things over for you with your father. What would you be doing?"

"Well, it's a dude ranch an' they let the dudes help take care of the cattle an' Sally tells me they've got some colts to start. When I was there last summer, it appeared to be a pretty well-run outfit. Dad sold them some replacement heifers a few years ago an' I saw some of those cows when I left last year. I guess it would be cattle, horses, an' dudes."

"That might make a fun summer job for you," replied Mother.

"Can you mail this package an' a letter when you go to town? I'll give you some money to handle it."

"Yes," said Mother.

I gave Mother a ten-dollar bill and admonished her, as she had done to me many times, "Bring me the change."

"Yes sir," replied Mother. "This should get to her by Christmas, if I can get it to the post office early enough."

I hadn't thought about it getting to Sally by Christmas. Just getting it to her was my main concern. I was learning that timing had a lot to do with things. "Thank you," I said. I went to my room to compose a letter to Sally to accompany the package. I didn't really know what to say, but I followed Mother's suggestion.

After supper, with the letter written, I went to bed.

The day before Christmas, I went out to the horse pasture with a halter for Charlie and a halter for Sassy. I caught Charlie, jumped on him bareback and rode the pasture until I found Matilda and Sassy. I thought I might have an easier time by leading Matilda and letting Sassy follow. The plan worked good and in no time we were in the barn.

I tied Charlie in a stall and tied Sassy in a stall next to him. Then I led Matilda back to the horse pasture and turned her loose. There was some snow on the ground and as I walked back to the ranch it started to snow.

A white Christmas will make Mother happy, I thought, as I traced Charlie's tracks in the snow. I knew that the chores would have to be done before any presents were opened in the morning.

When I got back to the house, I got some red crepe paper. I thought I would tie a ribbon around Charlie's and Sassy's neck to designate them as presents. Tommy and Betty would see them before we had our official present opening, but that would be all right.

Christmas morning came and Tommy was in a hurry to get the chores done and open presents. Betty was even more excited. My brother and sister discovered my presents for them out in the barn and their reaction was very pleasant. Betty was reluctant to leave Sassy and was persuaded to leave only when Dad told her there were more presents in the house that needed opening. The chores were done for the morning.

"Your gift sure made a hit with your brother and sister," said Dad as we walked to the house. "That might have made Betty's Christmas."

I couldn't wait to open Sally's present, although I tried to withhold my anticipation.

After a few presents were open, Mother suggested, "Why don't you open your present from Sally, son?"

Dad didn't show any surprise at Mother's mention of Sally. Apparently Mom had discussed my so-called girlfriend with him earlier.

Tommy showed some surprise. "You got a girlfriend?" He seemed amazed that I should have a girlfriend. He didn't have any problem meeting people and he was more outgoing than I was. It was rumored in school that he had a girlfriend or two.

"Yes son," said Dad, "lets see what your lady friend gave you."

I could feel the heat rising up my neck and onto my face as I picked up the package. It was a little heavier than I remembered and I began to wonder if the shirt I sent Sally was enough. Very deliberately, I unwrapped the present.

Inside I found a brand new breast collar, a pair of spurs with just the right size rowels and jingle bobs to boot, a new shirt, and a picture of Sally. I was overwhelmed and I knew that the shirt I sent Sally could not compare in quality or quantity with the gift she gave me. I immediately felt embarrassed and a little cheap in light of the gift I gave her, and the seasonal spirits I had experienced evaporated.

I was admiring Sally's picture when Mother said, "Let's see what your lady friend looks like."

Reluctantly, I passed the picture around.

"She's very pretty," said Mother. "This must be her school picture."

"You could do worse," said Dad. "I imagine you've got a lot of competition."

I immediately became concerned about the competition. I thought my gift would look pretty cheap in light of the other gifts she surely would have received from my competition.

A few more gifts were much-needed items—gloves with liners, new over boots, and a new scotch cap with ear muffs. All were needed and much appreciated.

One gift was particularly interesting. My dad received a set of long johns, the old-fashioned type all in one piece. It was a red flannel union suit, with buttons down the front and up the back. Dad said he hadn't seen any for a long time. He thought they stopped making them.

"Would you care to model them, Honey?" There was a certain amount of jest in Mother's voice.

"No," said Dad, as he held them up in front of him. "You don't always know what buttons are buttoned and which ain't."

"What did I get you?" I was curious to know what my presents were to Mother and Dad.

"That reminds me," said Dad, "Come help me get out presents, son."

I followed Dad out to the garage. Inside was a large cardboard box. I thought it was a new saddle.

"Give me a hand here, this is what you got your mother," said Dad, as he lifted one side of the box.

I got a hold underneath the box. It was heavier than a new saddle.

"What is it?" I asked.

"You'll find out."

We took the box into the living room. Mother had set up a table against one wall and we set the box on the table.

"Everyone gather around," said Dad. "Mother, do you want to do the honors?"

With a sharp knife, Mother carefully cut the box open and kept the sides up, with a little help from Dad. When she was done, she let the sides of the box fall down to reveal a new television. There were squeals of joy from Betty. We hadn't had one before. This was the present Tommy and Betty and I had got for my parents.

"Turn it on! Turn it on!" Betty was even more pleased with the television than she was with Sassy.

"We need to hook it up first, Betty. We'll get started on that as soon as we have something to eat," said Dad.

After a late breakfast, Dad, Tommy, and I went outside to hook up the antenna. Tommy and Dad are more mechanically inclined than I am, so my job was essentially to hold the ladder while they climbed up on the roof. I suppose I was really helpful going back and forth to the shop to get the various tools they needed.

With the antenna hooked up, the television was turned on and Dad promptly selected a football game to watch. The afternoon was spent watching the football game although Betty quickly lost interest in it and went to the barn to be with Sassy.

As she left the house, Dad said, "Yep, your present of that burro has made Betty's Christmas, son. She's headed out to be with her. You really handled this Christmas well, son. And you did it without even going to town! That's really being resourceful and doing some good planning. Even Tommy liked Charlie. He used him quite a bit last summer, and even told me he'd like to buy him from you."

"I didn't really plan it that way," I said, "that's just the way it turned out. I'm kinda glad it happened that way, it saved me some money. And Charlie's startin' to get a little age to him. Besides that, Roman's a better horse."

After the evening chores were done and supper was finished, Mother suggested that I might call my lady friend, Sally, and thank her for the wonderful gifts she had given me.

I thought about it, but declined. I didn't want to talk to Sally in front of everyone, although I thought it might be nice to talk to her. "I'll send her a nice long letter," I said. As of late, my letters, although I sent one every time I got one from her, had been getting shorter and shorter. I was running out of things to say, and most of it was just idle, meaningless talk.

The next morning before we started chores, Dad said, "We're going to try something new this winter. We'll start feeding in the evening, after you get home from school. I've been doing some reading and I understand up in Canada, they feed in the evening. Then most of their calves are born in the morning hours. That will make it easier on me during calving season; I might even be able to get a little more sleep."

"But I don't like the idea of loading the hay for feeding after dark," I said.

"You won't have to load the hay. I'll do that during the day," said Dad. "You boys can help me load the hay on the weekends."

Not having to load the hay during the week appealed to me. It seemed like we spent more time growing the hay, irrigating it, cutting it, hauling it, stacking it, and feeding it, than we spent with the cattle. Yet we were a cattle ranch. But the hay work came with the territory.

The new year came, and we all stayed up until midnight to welcome it in. It was a yearly event, although to me it was just another day.

School started the day after New Year's day. It was the same old routine, up early to do the chores, catch the bus to go to school, ride the bus home and do the chores. The only thing that was different was the feeding. I really liked feeding in the evening; it was a lot easier to throw the hay off the trailer than load it on the trailer, and I didn't have to help reload it.

I had written a long letter to Sally thanking her for the gifts and, not really having anything else to say, I expounded on the evening feeding we were trying out.

Sally's next letter was more complementary than the others. It started out;

My dear Loving, Thoughtful Cowboy,
   Thank you, thank you for the most beautiful blouse you sent me! I shall cherish it forever and it's so beautiful I might not even wear it. I never dreamed you had such exquisite tastes. Perhaps you are getting some social graces from your social studies class!

The rest of the letter went on to say what a wonderful Christmas she'd had. Her dad even came and spent some time with her during the holidays, leaving the ranch in Pat's capable hands. She closed with the reminder,

   Remember to contact Dad about your plans for the summer. He's counting on you to be there. So am I.
   Love,
   Sally

I was a little pleased that her greeting in the letter had been a little more friendly than her previous letters. The letter did remind me that I had to talk to my dad about my plans for the summer, and that I would have to improve my social graces. I was pretty sure I could go and I did want to see Sally again.

The next night, after we fed and during supper, I brought up the subject of my summer employment.

"Do you have any objections to my going to work for Bud Wilson this summer?"

"I guess not," said Dad. "What will you be doing?"

"Cattle, horses, an' dudes, I guess," I replied.

"How much does this new lady friend of yours have to do with this?"

I could feel my face starting to heat up as I started to blush. Sally wasn't a new lady friend, I'd met her last summer and we'd been corresponding all winter. "Not much, although I would like to see her in the shirt I bought her. You know, she called it a 'blouse' in her letter." I was trying to change the subject from my interest in this young lady to anything else.

"That's what it is, a blouse," said Mother. "And it is very pretty. You would have looked very silly wearing it to school."

"She said it was beautiful," I corrected.

"Bud Wilson called me a few weeks ago," said Dad.

"Does he want some more replacement heifers?"

"No, he called about you, wanting to know what your plans were," answered Dad.

"What did you tell him?"

"I told him I didn't know what your plans were, but that you are a big boy and can make your own plans. You pretty well proved that when you rode home from your old job last summer. Your mother has already talked to me and if you want to work for Bud, you better call him and let him know when you'll be there."

"Can I use the phone? It's a long distance call."

Every call from our ranch was a long distance call.

"Yep," was Dad's reply. "The number's written down inside the phone book."

I called Bud that night and hired on for the summer. I told Bud that I'd be there about a week after school let out as I'd have to ride my horse and use my burro for a pack animal. It would take a little time. That was all right with Bud.

In my next letter to Sally, I told her I would be showing up at the ranch about a week after school was out.

An Unexpected Rest

The rest of January was uneventful, although it was cold. February always suggested the coming of spring to me. It was the shortest month of the year and spring was right around the corner. Right behind February came March and the beginning of calving season.

I was helping Dad feed one night, and all of the sudden I felt a sharp pain in my side. Dad noticed me bent over on the trailer and not much hay being thrown off to the cattle.

"You ill, son?"

"I don't feel so hot," I said.

"You take it easy, I'll finish."

Tommy was driving the tractor. He had slowed down to see what was happening.

"Keep going, we've got to finish this then get to the house. This young hay feeder ain't feeling too good!"

Mother was immediately concerned when we reached the house. I could hardly straighten up.

Mother did a fairly thorough examination and said, "I think we need to take you to the hospital. I don't know what's wrong."

"It'll pass," I said. I sure hoped it would. I felt awful.

"I think we need to go right now," said Mother. There was a tone of urgency in her voice.

"Tommy, said Dad, "you're in charge. Don't stay up all night watching television. You and Betty be in bed by 9:30, or else. Your mother and I are going to town."

"Can we go?" Betty never wanted to miss a trip to town.

"No," said Dad, "and you better be in bed when I get home."

I stumbled out to the truck, with my dad steadying me on the way. I sat in the center while Dad drove. He did go a little fast for the snow-packed roads.

At the hospital, I was examined and the determination was made that I had acute appendicitis. I was wheeled into surgery, given a shot, and promptly went to sleep.

I woke up sometime later, how long I was under, I don't know. Mother was at my bedside, sleeping lightly.

I had some pain in my lower belly and groaned as I tried to roll over. At the sound of my groan, Mother woke up.

"How do you feel, son?"

I was still groggy from the operation. "I don't know."

"Well, you're minus your appendix now. Do you miss it?" Mother was trying to bring some humor into the situation. I didn't think it was very funny. I didn't even know I had one and now I didn't.

"Your father went home to take care of the kids. I'll call him and let him know you're all right. Get some rest."

As Mother left, a nurse entered and took my temperature.

"The doctor will be in to check on you in the morning," she said. The operation was a success."

I went back to sleep.

It was mid morning when I awoke. Mother and Dad were in my room.

"Looks like you'll get a few days off," said Dad. "You get to spend three days in bed here in the hospital. Then another three or four days of bed rest at home before you go back to school."

"That will be okay," I replied. "I've been thinking I've been working too hard anyways."

Mother and Dad left saying they'd be back in three days to pick me up. Mother promised she'd have a comfortable spot fixed up for me so I could watch television during the day.

I thought I would have a few days of peaceful bed rest in the hospital, but the nurse came in and made me get out of bed and walk around so I wouldn't get stiff. It was painful and I thought my new stitches were pulling out. The nurse assured me they weren't, but she made me walk around for half an hour.

The next day I managed to put on my pants and a shirt and walk to the hospital gift shop and I bought some stationery, some envelopes, and some stamps. The only stationery I could buy had the hospital's name and logo on it. I didn't think much of it, but it was all that was available. I went back to my bed and composed a long letter to Sally, but didn't tell her I was in the hospital. I didn't think it was important; I was going home tomorrow anyway.

Before I left the hospital, I mailed the letter.

I spent the next couple of days resting at home. My teachers had sent some schoolwork home with Tommy and it didn't take long to complete it and get fairly caught up. I found it difficult to get interested in the daytime television soap operas, and was anxious to get out of the house, even if it meant going to school. After a few days, I was allowed to help feed, although I could only drive the tractor. The doctor had said I was not to do any heavy work until I was completely healed, probably for a month or so.

I received a letter from Sally a few days earlier than what had become regular. Her letters usually arrived on Mondays, but this one came on Thursday.

I wondered what had caused the change.

The letter started out,

My dear Jerk,

I was used to that, we were on familiar terms. It continued,

> *What has happened out there? You wrote to me on hospital stationery. And an extraordinary long letter at that. I have been worried sick wondering if you are all right. You need to call me and let me know if everything is okay.*

She wrote her phone number and continued to write, complaining to me how inconsiderate I was by making her worry like I did. From the urgency of her letter, I thought I had better answer her pretty quick. I knew a phone call would be out of the question, every call from the ranch was a long distance call and we only had the phone for emergencies. Besides that, I really didn't want to call; I figured all the talk would be about me. I guess I'm a little bashful.

That night after supper, I wrote a letter to Sally explaining that I'd had my appendix removed, I really didn't know how they did it, I was asleep all the time, but so far I didn't miss it at all. I did mention that I didn't think it was a big deal. I told her I couldn't call because all the phone calls from our ranch were long distance calls. I hoped she would understand.

I mailed the letter the next day from school. Without thinking, I had used the hospital stationery and envelope. It wasn't until after I had put it in the outgoing mail that I realized it, and considered rewriting it on school stationery, but decided against it. It was already written and on its way. I didn't think it would cause any further problems, I had explained that I was all right.

Horseback Again

My operation was forgotten during the next couple of months and I got back into the routine of school and chores.

Calving season was approaching and Dad had already brought the horses into the corrals so they would be handy when needed. He wanted to grain them a little before we started using them on a regular basis. They would be used pretty hard during the calving season.

The horses had wintered well. We had fed a little hay to them just to help keep them in shape. It was still cold and not all of the snow had melted.

I wondered if Roman would buck with his first saddling of the year. I knew the other horses probably wouldn't, and I guessed Roman wouldn't, but I didn't know.

The days were getting longer and it was nice to feed with some daylight still showing. It was also getting a little warmer.

We did the feeding as soon as I got home from school. Dad explained to me that, "We could look at the cows as we were feeding, and if anything looked like it was going to calve real quick, we'd come back on the horses and move the cow to one of the corrals by the barn. Then if she needed help, she'd be close to the house and we could help her if necessary. A day or two after the cow had calved and we'd ear-tagged the calf, we'd put the new mother and her calf in a separate pasture. Every now and then, we'd have to rope the new calves that were born on the feeding grounds and ear-tag them, then, on the weekends, we'd gather the cows that had calved and move them to the new pasture."

I liked the idea. It meant some riding during the week and a lot of riding during the weekends. It was becoming more difficult to concentrate on schoolwork with the cow work taking precedence at the home ranch.

Every morning, before I left for school, I admonished my Dad, "Make sure you leave some calves for me to ear-tag on the weekend!"

"There'll be some for you," Dad would reply, grinning. He knew I loved to rope. "Are you sure you can rope missing your appendix? If you can't, Tommy and I will have to do it all."

"I believe I'll be fine. And I believe I can still out-rope both you and Tommy!" There was some good-natured rivalry between the three of us regarding our cowboy skills. I knew I could rope better than Tommy, but my dad was pretty good and I wasn't sure if I could out rope him. But I was going to act like I was better than him, even if I wasn't.

I didn't have to ride out to bring in any cows that might need help after school, although Dad had brought in one cow that he thought might need some help. The first Saturday after we started calving, we saddled our horses to go ear-tag new calves.

Roman had a hump in his back as I tightened the cinch. I didn't really know what to expect, I'd just got him last summer and had used him pretty regular. I'd never saddled him up after turning him out all winter.

"Better untrack him and get on him in the round corral," said Dad. He'd been watching, with the practiced eye of an experienced cowboy and stockman.

"That's just what I'm plannin' on doin'," I answered.

I led Roman to the round corral and watched him out of the corner of my eye as we walked. He was walking kinda gingerly, and I didn't know if he was going to blow up or not. Inside the round corral, I led him around to the right a few times and then around to the left. I wasn't in a rush.

Dad and Tommy were on their horses outside the corral, watching.

"Hurry an' get on," said Tommy. He was getting impatient. "If you don't get going soon, those calves will be weaned an' we won't know which calves belong to which cows!"

Dad smiled. "He should be all right now. Get on."

I tightened the cinch, turned Roman around again, put my foot on the stirrup and swung on the horse.

"Don't pull out your stitches," said Tommy, as I settled in the saddle. I laughed at the comment; the stitches from my appendix operation had long since been removed.

I rocked the saddle from side to side and felt the muscles in Roman's back tighten. I figured he was going to buck. I touched him with a spur and he took a big jump forward and stopped. I touched him again and he jumped forward again, although not as high or as far.

"We'll be all day doin' this, one jump at a time," said Tommy. "Dig him good an' let's get goin'!"

Dad laughed. "Just ease him into it, son. The horse doesn't know what he wants to do. Don't rush him."

I touched him again with a spur, and he jumped forward again, although not as high or as far. A few more jumps and

Roman started to walk out. I walked him around the corral a few times and when he settled down, I moved him into a trot. He did it without offering to buck.

"Open the gate," I said. "I think he's ready now."

Dad swung the gate open from horseback. "Let's head out!"

We started out toward the feed grounds at an easy trot to save time.

There were a few calves on the ground, all of them needing ear-tags. The plan was to rope the calves, hold them down until their mother showed up, then put a tag in their ear with a number on it that corresponded to the mother's tag. We'd have to write the mother's tag number on the calf's tag when the mother showed up.

We'd have to be kinda careful; some of the cows were very protective of their calves.

Dad roped the first calf, and I got the job of doing the ear-tagging. Tommy, riding Charlie, stayed between the mother cow and the calf and me while I wrote the number on the tag and put the tag in the calf's ear. It was a pretty simple procedure. I would put the calf on his side and hold him down while I wrote the number on the tag and pierced his ear. I was hindered a little as I had to hold Roman's reins. I didn't hobble him as I knew the whole operation would only take about a minute.

Tommy roped the second calf, and Dad did the ear-tagging. I roped the third calf on my second try, I'd missed the first loop, and Dad once again did the ear-tagging.

Roman jumped to the side and started to run off when I threw my first loop as if it surprised him, but he didn't offer to buck. I pulled him in as I coiled my rope.

"One, one, and two," said Tommy as Dad let the calf up.

34

I asked, although I already knew the answer, "What's that mean?"

"It means Dad's got one, I've got one, an' you've got two. We're keeping score an' right now you're losin'. Low score wins."

"It don't help when my horse has forgotten everything he knows," I said.

There was a good deal of rivalry between Tommy and I and a little of it spilled over to Dad. We were all quite proud of our cowboy skills although Dad knew he was a good hand and didn't have to prove it to anyone. Tommy and I were still trying to out do each other.

Dad roped the next calf and Tommy snagged the next one. I caught one on the second loop again.

"Two, two, and four," said Tommy. "You're startin' to get a little behind."

"I've been sick," I said. I was digging a little deep for excuses. "My stay in the hospital didn't help much, and I only have enough excuses for one miss." I saw my Dad grinning at my answer. He was enjoying this competition between his sons.

Dad caught another calf and Tommy finally missed one. I managed to catch one on the first loop. After Tommy missed his calf, he wasn't so vocal about keeping score. We finished the ear-tagging before noon and rode back to the ranch for our noon meal.

"What's the score now, Tommy?"

"Dad didn't miss any, you missed three, an' I forgot what I did," he replied.

"You missed four," I said. I had been quietly keeping track.

"It'll be kinda tough for you kids to keep up with the old man," said Dad. "Maybe, when you're my age, you might be as good as I am. But you'll have to rope as many calves as I have. It'll take you a little time." Dad had to join in the rivalry, just to remind us kids that he was a top hand.

We went out again on Sunday and ear-tagged the calves that had been born that morning. One cow was particularly protective of her calf and Dad had a tough time keeping her away from me as I ear-tagged the calf. At one point she almost tipped Dad and his horse, Buster, over. Tommy was enjoying the show, not paying any attention to what I was doing.

"You ought to rope that cow and keep her away from Dad an' me," I said. By the time Tommy built a loop to catch the cow, I had finished the ear-tagging and turned the calf loose. The cow didn't present a threat anymore.

The rest of the spring passed. The calving went on, although Dad did bring a few cows in that needed help with the birthing process. I didn't have to ride through the cattle after we had fed, my riding only came on the weekends, when Dad, Tommy, and I would go out and ear-tag the calves.

Roman was getting used to being rode again and he didn't flinch when I saddled him and we moved out to the feed grounds. The few months rest had done him some good and he was becoming the good horse I knew he was.

March passed and April brought sunny weather. Tommy and I entered the team roping at the local school rodeo. Dad decided to take the whole family to town for the rodeo, hauling our horses in a trailer. Tommy and I rode in the back of the truck, giving up our positions in the cab to Mother and Betty.

It wasn't a pleasant ride into town in the back of the truck. It was dusty and dirty.

At the rodeo, Tommy missed his throw at the head. I was supposed to be the heeler, but I went ahead and caught the head.

Tommy missed his throw at the heels and our efforts resulted in a "no time." But we had fun.

After our failed attempt in the team roping, we left our horses at the rodeo grounds and went into town so Mother could do some shopping. We had supper in town, went back to the rodeo grounds, loaded our horses and headed for home.

The ride home was just as dirty and dusty as the ride into town. Tommy slept most of the way; I never could understand how he could sleep almost anywhere.

Social Graces

The weekly correspondence to Sally continued. With the coming of calving season and having to ear-tag the calves, my letters became longer as I had something to write about, describing my roping adventures with Tommy and Dad. Her letters took on a more upbeat tone; she was looking to get back to the ranch for the summer. She did say that,

> *You might be better at roping than I am because you've been able to practice all spring.*

The subject changed abruptly when she asked,

> *Have you learned anything about social graces in your social studies class?*

I'd plumb forgot about learning how to square dance, and I had promised myself I'd do that during the winter. That night, after supper, I asked Mother, "Do you know how to dance?"

"Certainly," was her reply. "Why?"

"Do you know how to dance good enough that you could teach me?"

"Of course. Why do you want to learn?"

"I was thinking it might be good to know in case I have to intermingle with the dudes this summer." I didn't want to tell Mother that I was planning on dancing with Sally and wanted to make it sound like it was business.

Mother gave me an all-knowing look and said, "I'll teach you right after I get these dishes done."

"Do you want some help?"

Mother's all-knowing look changed to a look of surprise, or maybe it was shock. I'd never volunteered to help with the dishes before.

"No," she said, "you set up the phonograph player on the kitchen table. I'm about done here and then I'll get some records.

The dishes were done and Mother had put some records on the phonograph, then she turned to me.

"You take my left hand and hold it in your right hand," said Mother.

I did as I was told.

"Hold it good so she can't slap you when you step on her feet!" Tommy had entered the room.

"Mind your own business, Tommy!" Mom said.

"I'd slap you a good one if I wasn't holdin' Mom's hand," I said.

"Now, put your right arm around my waist and I'll put my left arm on your shoulder. Yes, that's right. Now just start moving, keeping time to the music. Lead the girl with your left arm. That's right. Good!"

"Oops," I said. I had stepped on her foot.

"Don't take such long steps. Just glide your feet along the floor. That's right. One, two, one two."

"Sorry," I said. I stopped, I'd stepped on her foot again.

"Don't stop. Keep going. A good dancer will learn to keep her feet out from under yours. Your father walked all over my feet years ago. I thought I'd never get over it."

We continued around the room, with Mother offering encouragement and gently showing me how to lead by moving my arm around. I was starting to get the hang of it.

"You do have some rhythm," said Mother. "You keep practicing and you'll be pretty good."

After about half an hour, we stopped. I was just getting the hang of it and we were quitting.

"We'll do a little more after supper tomorrow night. You know how your horses learn, a little at a time. We'll teach you just like you teach your horses," said Mother.

"I wish they'd do that in school," I said.

I went to my room, closed the door, and did some practicing with an imaginary partner until it was time to go to bed. I thought I was doing pretty good.

The next night, we had another session after supper. I didn't step on Mother's feet as much and thought I had made some progress. As we were finishing up, I asked Mother, "What about square dancing?"

"We can work on that tomorrow," she said. "What we've been doing is called the two-step. You can use it to almost any kind of music. You might have to help with the dishes tomorrow, as payment."

"I can do that," I answered.

The next night we worked on square dancing. Mother convinced Tommy and Betty to help and although we didn't have any music or a caller, Mom went through all the moves and demonstrated them and had me practice them with Tommy and Betty. She even called the moves by their names as we did them.

At least I know what a Do-Si-Do is, I thought.

"Remember," she said, "it's really important to know your right from your left when you're square dancing."

"I know," I said, remembering the square dancing last summer at the Wilson ranch. I was embarrassed and resolved that I wouldn't be embarrassed again this summer.

"How do you know?"

"I guess I'm a fast learner," I said. "Why do they call it a square dance when all they do is go around in circles?"

Mother just laughed and I went to my room.

I did some practicing on my own in my bedroom every night after supper. I thought I could do all right and only needed more practice, but I really didn't have anyone to practice with. I didn't want to practice too much with Mother—I was getting tired of helping with the dishes.

I got a lot of practice dancing, but didn't really know where to go to learn how to kiss and to get some practice at doing that.

An Unwelcome Visitor

School continued, and the dancing lessons continued after supper each night. I didn't think I needed them, but Mother insisted, saying, "Practice makes perfect." I really think she was enjoying the help I was giving her in doing the dishes each night. I was getting really good at doing the dishes, and showing some improvement at doing the two-step.

One day I came home from school and noticed that the trailer wasn't loaded and the cows weren't fed. I looked in the barn thinking maybe Dad had to pull a calf and maybe he needed some help, but he wasn't there. I went to the house looking for him.

"Where's Dad, Mom?"

"He had a chore to do. I expect him back anytime."

"The hay's not loaded an' we've got to feed. I'll get Tommy an' we'll get started. I wonder where he went, the truck's in the yard."

"He went out on Buster," said Mother.

I didn't know what was up, but thought it must be pretty serious. Tommy and I loaded the trailer, fed the cows, and did the evening chores.

At supper, it was obvious that Mother was becoming very concerned. When I volunteered to do the dishes, Mother didn't accept my offer, saying, "I need to stay busy."

The dishes were done, schoolwork was done. All that remained to be done was to wait for Dad to show up. An hour passed and Dad still hadn't showed up. Mother sent Betty to bed and after another half an hour, Tommy went to bed.

After another half an hour passed, Mother said, "Shouldn't you be going to bed?"

"I probably ought to wait up for Dad," I said. "If I knew where he went, I'd go look for him, just in case he needs some help. Where did he go?"

"I don't know. He saddled Buster, got his rifle and left. He did say, 'Don't wait up for me.' I don't know where he went."

"What did he get the rifle for?"

"I don't know," answered Mother.

An hour or so later, I fell asleep on the couch watching the television.

Around one o'clock in the morning, I heard the front door open. Mother was already greeting Dad. He looked tired.

"Where have you been? I've been worried sick," said Mother.

I was fully awake now.

"What are you doing up at this hour, son? And on a school night to boot."

"I was waiting for you," I said.

"Well," said Dad, "I've been kinda busy. I saw some cougar tracks out on the feed ground, and when I went to feed the cows that had already calved out, I saw the critter. He'd killed one of our calves, and was dragging him off when I saw him. I finished feeding, got Buster and my rifle and started trailing him.

"I was gaining on him; I don't think he even knew I was following him. I finally caught up to him about fifteen miles south, by the head of Willow Creek. He hadn't finished eating the calf; I'd come across parts of the calf earlier on the trail. He was lying on a rock when I spotted him and I think he saw me at the same time that I saw him.

"I tied Buster to a tree and hobbled him. You know how he is when there's shooting, and then I got the rifle and got a shot at the lion."

I knew how Buster was. Dad had shot a deer when we were out hunting one year, and at the sound of the gunshot, Buster had run off. Charlie had to carry Dad and me double for a couple of miles until we found Buster.

"My first shot at the lion, he was running by now, broke his back. But he kept going, dragging his hindquarters. They must have a lot of strength on their forequarters to drag their hindquarters like that. It made an easy trail to follow, there's still quite a bit of snow up there.

"After another mile or so, I saw him again and I finished him off. I just left him there. I'll go back and skin him out tomorrow. Can I borrow your burro to carry the hide home?"

"Sure," I said. "Her pack saddle is hangin' in the barn. I'll even go with you and help!"

"Not with school tomorrow. I can do that job by myself. Now you need to be off to bed, young man. It's way past your bedtime. Is it too late to get some supper at this establishment? I haven't had anything to eat all day."

"I'll have to heat up your supper," said Mother. "I tried to keep it warm, but decided to put it away. If I'd have kept it warmed up, it would be as tough as old shoe leather by now."

"We did all the chores, other than load the hay for tomorrow's feeding. You've been doin' that while we were in school," I said.

"I can handle that before I go get the lion. How would you like a nice mountain lion rug, Mother? I know where there's one just waiting for us. It would look pretty nice lying on the floor next to our bed."

"It would look nicer hanging on the wall in the hall," replied Mother.

"Whatever you want. I'll ride Sugar out to get the cat. Buster's had a pretty rough day today."

"I wonder if that's the cat that tried to get Sassy last summer. He pert near got her, but a sheep rancher showed up and took a few shots at him an' run him off."

"You didn't tell us about that," said Dad. "But it's past your bedtime, you tell us about it later. Get to bed!"

I hadn't thought about the mountain lion incident all winter, being concerned with school and Sally and everything else. I did remember that the sheep rancher was Bud Wilson's brother, but didn't remember hearing his first name. I got to wondering where he wintered his sheep herd and how he made it through the winter. I thought I ought to make a mental note to ask Bud about it, but decided to write it down instead. My mental notes weren't helping as my school grades weren't improving.

The next day, after Tommy and I helped feed, we all admired the hide of the cougar that was laid out on the corral fence. The hide actually looked bigger than the cat that had attacked Sassy.

Dad was saying, "We haven't had much of a problem with

mountain lions around here for quite a few years. I was really surprised to see this one the other day. But he won't be getting any of our calves anymore. Tomorrow I'll take him into town and have that hide tanned.

"Sugar sure didn't want to get close to that cougar, but your burro walked right up to him. She might be fairly handy to have around."

It occurred to me that Dad's late arrival the night before had got me out of doing the dishes, but Mother hadn't forgotten.

"Get the dishes done, and we'll have another dance lesson."

"Mom, I'm really feeling pretty good about my dancin'," I said, trying to get out of doing the dishes.

"Dancing is something you can't ever get too good at. And you're certainly no Arthur Murray."

The phonograph was set up and another dancing lesson began, after I did the dishes.

While we were dancing, I asked Mother, "What do I do if a girl puts her head on my shoulder?"

"Get a good hold on her," said Tommy, "she's probably fixin' to fall asleep. Hold her real good so she don't fall down!"

"Tommy!" Mother was a little stern with her reprimand.

Tommy had become a frequent observer during our dancing lessons and even got to try a few steps with Mother every now and then. However, he never helped with the dishes.

May arrived. We'd stopped feeding, having turned the cows into a separate pasture close to the house. We were pretty well calved out and Dad picked a weekend in the middle of May to do the branding. The beginning of May also meant there was only about a month of school left, and I was getting anxious to head out and get started on my summer job. I was also getting anxious to see Sally again.

Our branding went well. Dad had invited some relatives to help as he did every year. Uncles, cousins, and a few friends all helped. Mother and Betty were pretty busy cooking, with help from a couple of aunts. There was a pretty big crew to fix a noon meal for. And then there was supper to prepare. Our branding generally was a two-day affair.

Dad, Tommy, and I gathered the cows and calves and had them in the corrals when the help showed up. The three of us handled the roping alternately switching, taking turns. Some of the relatives also got a chance to rope. I wasn't really keeping track, but Tommy appeared to be. While Dad was roping, Tommy came up to me and said, grinning, "Dad just missed one. That's the first one he's missed all day."

I asked him, "How many have you missed?"

"You've missed two," he said.

Feeling a little irritated at Tommy for keeping track of everybody's roping, I asked him again, "How many have you missed?" I stressed the "you" making sure he knew I was asking about him and not Dad or me.

"I've missed four," he replied, sheepishly.

"That's all right," I said. "We've got a lot more to do and you'll probably miss a few more."

Tommy gave me a dirty look and went back to what he was doing.

It was an all-day job, and when the sun went down we still weren't done. Preparations were made to provide sleeping arrangements for everyone. Some of the relatives had brought camp trailers and they slept in them.

The next day went pretty much like the first day of branding, although some of the city relatives complained that they had forgotten they had some muscles that they hadn't used since the year before.

When the branding was done, we trailed the cattle to the spring range. It wasn't a long cattle drive, just to the east boundary of our ranch, where we turned them loose. There might be a late calf or two, but they'd be all right. The snow had melted, the grass was coming up, and the cattle would do all right for a month or so. Dad and Tommy would gather them and move them onto the summer range about the end of June. I felt a little guilty about leaving the work to them, but it wouldn't be all that difficult.

A week before school let out for the summer, I sent a letter to Sally, explaining that I would be riding my horse and bringing my pack burro to her dad's ranch and there weren't any post offices along the way and I didn't know exactly what day, but I would be showing up about a week after I left our ranch.

I began bringing Matilda to the barn and brushing her every day after school. She hadn't shed off too well and I wanted her to look good when I showed up at the Wilson ranch. Betty noticed this and began to bring Sassy in and brush her.

"You really need to help me, Sis," I said. "Sassy already looks good, but her mom is needin' a little assistance."

"No," Betty agreed, "she's not as pretty as she could be."

Betty began to bring some hair conditioner with her when she brushed Sassy and in no time Sassy was shining.

Matilda was beginning to look better, but she didn't compare to Sassy. I thought perhaps it was because she was getting old.

Dad had the farrier come out and shoe all the horses, including Roman.

"Do you want the donkey shod? I think I've got some small pony shoes that will fit her."

"No," I replied. "She went barefoot all last summer, she'll be all right."

Under the watchful eye of the farrier, I trimmed Matilda's feet. I think I did it because Matilda was so short, and the farrier wanted to save his back. When I got done, I was wishing he'd done it.

On the Trail Again

The day after school was out for the summer, I went to town with Mother. I thought it might be a good idea to get some new clothes and a new hat. I thought it would be a good idea to look a little nicer for the dudes during the summer. I could wear my old clothes on the trip to the Wilson's.

I also bought enough groceries for a week. I'd had plenty of beef stew the summer before, and tried to vary the items, but canned beef stew was a staple. I made sure I had toilet paper. I'd forgot it last summer and regretted it.

I assembled the gear I'd need for the ride down to the Wilson's when we got home. I packed them in the panniers that night, making sure I had the weight in each pannier as even as possible. I double-checked everything to make sure I hadn't forgotten anything like I did when I left the old job last summer. I planned on leaving the next morning, as early as possible. I didn't know if I was anxious to see Sally or anxious to get going.

"Make sure you write at least once a week." Mother was helping me. "Let us know what you're doing and how you're getting along."

"I'll probably be too busy to write much," I said.

"But you found time to write to Sally," Mother countered.

"I did that during school." I let the cat out of the bag. "During study hall when I'd got caught up with school work." I tried to recover quickly.

"If you found time to write letters in school, you can certainly find time to write your family!"

"I don't really know what I'd say," I said.

"You could let us know what you're doing and how you're doing. You could tell us about the guests and how you're getting along with them. You could also tell us how you're getting along with your young lady friend. You did say you had some competition. We'd be most interested in learning about that and her."

I bet you'd like to know more than I'm willing to tell, I thought to myself. And I didn't want to be saddled with extra domestic chores on this job.

"That sounds like a pretty tall order," I said. "Remember I'm working for them, not reporting on them. However, I will try." I was trying to end this conversation as politely as possible.

"I know, I know," replied Mother. "But I do worry about you when you're gone. You're fairly mature, but you're not a full-grown man yet."

"I know," I said, "but I'm closer to it than you are!"

Mother chuckled and left the room.

I carried the panniers down to the barn so I'd be ready to leave in the morning. I had a strange sensation of regretting leaving, missing the family and such, but an undeniable sensation of excitement, heading out for new adventures. I didn't really know what to expect.

That evening was spent visiting with the family after supper.

51

A good part of the evening was spent listening to Dad admonishing me about what to do and what not to do.

The next morning, I saddled Roman and Matilda, got Matilda loaded and rode to the house. Tommy and Dad saddled their horses also.

"We'll ride as far as the end of the spring pasture with you," said Dad. "We can check the cows on the way back."

"Aren't you going to use your new breast collar?" Mother had it with her on the front porch.

"Yep," I said. "I wanted it to look good when I showed up at the Wilson's."

I looped Matilda's lead rope around my saddle horn and took the breast collar from Mother.

"I'd appreciate it if you'd put this in my room," I said, as I handed my old breast collar to her and put the new one on my horse. "I might need it later."

I gave Mother and Betty a kiss goodbye.

"You be a good boy," said Mother, "that is, young man!"

"Yes," I said, getting on Roman. Giving Matilda a jerk on her lead rope, I said, "Come on Sally, you old hussy! Ah, that is, ah, Matilda."

I'd changed Sally's name to Matilda last fall and hadn't been around her enough to get accustomed to the name change. *I'll have to work on that,* I thought.

I turned Roman toward the barn where Tommy and Dad were waiting, gave Matilda another jerk on her lead rope and started out.

"Hurry up," said Tommy. He was always in a rush.

One last wave to Mother and Betty, and I was off.

The ride through the spring pasture was leisurely with Dad

reminding me of his admonitions from the night before. His last admonition was, "Make sure you put your fires out good!"

We reached the end of our spring pasture and Tommy opened the gate for me. I said, "So long," shook hands with Dad and Tommy and I was off.

One final wave as I topped the ridge and they were out of sight. I was on my own.

Not too long after I left Tommy and Dad, I came across some strange looking ground, around the head of Willow Creek. It looked like an animal had died, as there was evidence of entrails having been scattered around. At first I thought that a deer had died there, but there wasn't any hair or hide around. Then I remembered the mountain lion Dad had shot during the winter. Maybe this is where he shot him?

Dad had told me about where he had shot the lion, and this area fit the description.

The ride through our summer pasture was leisurely. I noticed the grass was coming; it looked like there would be plenty. There was still some snow up on the higher ridges and there was a little snow in the shady lower areas. In early afternoon, I started to think about making a camp. I sure didn't want to be camping in the snow and trying to start a fire with wet wood.

I found a nice spot along Cottonwood Creek. The creek ran into the river that went through our ranch. I knew this part of the country well. There was plenty of grass for Roman and Matilda and plenty of busted tree limbs for firewood. I made camp early, hobbled my animals and gave them some grain. They shouldn't go too far during the night. I built a big fire, opened a can of beef stew and ate supper. It was good, but all too soon to become a familiar reminder of last summer's trip. I considered opening up a second can, but decided on a can of peaches instead. I lingered around camp early that afternoon, and put in a bigger supply of firewood. It would be colder at night than when I came through here last summer.

Sleep came easy that night, listening to the coyotes howl. I always enjoyed hearing them.

I was up early the next morning, before the sun, and got a fire built fast. It was cold! I got the coffee going and couldn't wait for it to get done. I needed something to help warm me up. When the coffee was finally ready, it seemed like it took all morning, it was real comforting to warm my hands on the cup and let the coffee warm my insides.

As the sun came up, I started to warm up. I found Roman and Matilda not too far from camp. I brought them into camp, grained them and got them saddled. I loaded Matilda, reluctantly put out the fire, stuffed my coffee cup in a pannier, got on Roman and started out. Matilda was reluctant to start, but a hard jerk on her lead rope convinced her it was time to go.

I enjoyed riding during the next couple of days. I had settled into a familiar routine: break camp in the morning, ride for a while, sometimes take a mid-morning break, ride until early afternoon, take a break and have some peaches or tomatoes, then ride until late afternoon, make camp and settle in for the night. I was used to the routine, it had become established during the previous summer when I rode my horse home.

The ride during the day could have been extremely boring, but I kept busy watching the country. Traveling horseback, a feller doesn't miss much if he keeps his eyes open. I saw a lot of deer and even a few fawns. Occasionally I would see a badger and in the pine trees, an occasional pine martin and once a weasel, the tip of his tail still white. There were a lot of sage hens.

Embarrassment

Often, as I was riding, I would wonder what the early trappers and pioneers experienced as they first entered this part of the country. In some places there were some pretty deep gulches and arroyos to get across. Every now and then it was difficult for Roman, and I could only imagine how tough it would have been for the pioneers and their wagons. And I had the benefit of the map that Bud had drawn for me last summer. The pioneers didn't have the benefit of any maps.

In a couple of days, I reached the Peterson Ranch. I came across some of their hands moving cattle. I had met some of them last summer when I rode through their property to get home. I hoped my crossing their property wouldn't cause them or me any problems. Once again, I was invited to stay with them at the ranch house, but I declined.

I had been camping at about the same places I'd camped last summer on the way home. I figured I would need about three days to reach the Wilson ranch and staying at the Peterson place might put me just a little late. I didn't want to show up after dark. It would be difficult to get settled and the cook would insist on fixing me supper. It would be easier to show up along about mid-afternoon. Besides that, I was anxious to see Sally. I was sure the Peterson's didn't have any girls as cute as Sally.

I became increasingly anxious as the days passed and I got closer to the Wilson's. I wondered if Sally would already be there or if I would get there before she did. How would she act when she saw me? How would I act when I saw her? What would I say? How would I greet her? A big kiss? I hadn't any practice doing that. And what about her boyfriend?'

A lot of questions entered my mind as I rode and I didn't know how to answer any of them. I was getting a little nervous. I made what I figured to be my last camp and took a little more time setting it up. I was trying to find answers to my questions.

The next morning, I was up early. I put on the new clothes I had got in town before I left. I took some extra time washing my face. I did want to look presentable when I got to the ranch. As I ran my hand over my face, the thought came to me, *Maybe I ought to start shaving!* I could feel the peach fuzz on my cheeks. I hadn't thought to bring a razor, and didn't really know how to use one anyway.

I got as clean as I could, got saddled and packed and on the way. Around noon, I started to get a funny feeling in my stomach and even had some thoughts about turning around and going home to help Dad. But I couldn't go back—I didn't have enough groceries to make it home. I was really getting nervous and a little scared.

We didn't stop for a mid-morning break, but lingered a little longer at our midday meal. I knew this part of the Wilson ranch and thought I should get to the ranch house around three o'clock, taking my time. I was in a rush, but didn't want to rush too much.

I rode through the yard at the Wilson ranch and was surprised that no one was around. There had always been some people around in the past. I rode to the barn and found Patrick inside oiling a saddle.

"Well, howdy!" He stuck his hand out. "It's good to see you. We figured you'd be showin' up in the next day or two."

I shook his hand. It was good to see him. "How'd you winter? You look pretty fit to me."

"Get down off your horse an' visit awhile. Winter wasn't bad. There's been some colder. Just an average winter, I suppose. How'd school treat you?"

"School treats me good enough, but not often enough," I said. "I'm glad it's over. What's new around here?"

"We've had a little bad luck. We lost some calves to a mountain lion this spring. Bud's horse slipped an' fell on some ice. Bud couldn't clear his stirrup fast enough an' busted his ankle. Bud's still in a cast. He was on crutches, but he's gettin' around usin' a cane now. It'll be awhile before he does any ridin'. None of the dudes have showed up yet. Misses Abercrombie, you met her last year, she's comin' tomorrow, goin' to spend the whole summer like she does every year.

"Tie up your horse an' donkey an' come up to the lodge. Bud will be wantin' to see you, maybe some other folks, too. We can take your donkey up to the bunkhouse an' unload her later. I'll give you a hand."

"What other folks? Still got the same cook?" I was hoping Patrick was referring to Sally, but didn't want to come right out and ask if she was here.

"You'll know some of them," said Patrick, smiling. "We do have a new hand or two."

We walked up to the lodge, talking about the past winter and it was all I could do to keep from asking, "Where's Sally? Is she here yet?"

"Oh, by the way, my Dad shot a mountain lion over on our place last winter," I said.

"Probably the same one that got our calves. Bud will be glad to hear that."

"As soon as his hide's tanned, he's goin' to be hangin' on our wall in the hallway," I said.

"That's a good place for him!"

As we walked up the stairs to the porch, Bud came out. He was limping, using a cane for support. He had a walking cast on his foot.

I put my hand out to greet him, but he brushed it aside and gave me a bear hug. I'm not used to being hugged by men and immediately felt uncomfortable. I'm not even used to being hugged by women.

"I'm sure glad you're here, young man. How are you doing?"

Before I could answer, he continued, "Maybe we can get some peace and quiet around here now. Every day for the last week, its been continual questions, 'Do you think he'll be here to-day?' or 'When's he getting here? I wish he'd hurry.' Now maybe this will end and we can get some work done around here."

Bud turned toward the house and yelled, "Sally! Come here, you've got a gentleman caller!"

"Actually," I said, "I come here to work." I didn't want anyone to know how anxious I was to see Sally.

"I'm right here!" she squealed as she ran out the door and right toward me. I put my hands up in self defense, but not quick enough. She had me in a bear hug and was kissing my face. I hadn't been slobbered on like that since she kissed me goodbye last summer.

I could hear Bud and Patrick laughing and see, out of the corner of my eye, Patrick bent over in laughter, holding his stomach.

When she finally backed off a little, probably just to catch her breath, I did manage to say, "It's nice to see you."

"It's so nice to see you," she said. Then she started kissing me again. She was not at all bashful in front of her father and Patrick, although I was feeling the heat from my blushing. I didn't really know what to do.

When she backed off again, she asked, "So, how do you like it?"

"What?" I asked.

"You didn't notice?"

"I really didn't have a chance," I said. "Notice what?"

"I'm wearing the blouse you bought me for Christmas! Isn't it darling? This is the first chance I've had to wear it. How did you know my size?"

"I just guessed," I said. I sure wasn't going to tell her I bought it by mistake. I couldn't believe anyone would make such a fuss over a shirt.

"It does look nice on you," I said. It looked nicer on her than it would have looked on me!

"You're looking good," I said.

"And so are you," she said. "You're not nearly as dirty as you were when you showed up last year."

Sally certainly wasn't bashful about speaking her mind. I was glad I had taken some extra time to clean up this morning and put on my new clothes.

"I did take a shower … last week," I said.

"Come in here," said Bud, as he pulled Sally into the lodge before she could pounce on me again. I followed them into the lodge, wiping the slobber off my face onto my sleeve.

"Wiping my kisses off, huh?" Sally noticed my wiping action.

"No," I said. "I just ain't used to havin' 'em on my nose, eyes, forehead an' cheek. I probably need to practice on this some."

"I expect you'll get plenty of practice later," she said.

In the lodge, we sat and visited. Bud filled me in on what was expected of me this summer, how many dudes were going to show up, and about how often we'd have to brand calves. "What with me being laid up, this foot is slow to heal; you and Pat will have to handle most of it. Of course Sally will be here to help. There's not much she can't do."

I knew Sally could do about anything, I was already aware of that. I'd already seen her rope.

Bud was really pleased to hear that my dad had shot a mountain lion. "Probably the one that got our calves. They have a pretty big range, something like two hundred fifty or three hundred square miles. They cover a lot of ground. Your dad did us all a big favor."

I was getting a little restless visiting, and I still had to take care of my horse and burro. "I probably ought to go unsaddle my horse and burro," I said, as I got up to leave. "I do have some canned goods I can give to the cook."

"I'll come and help," said Sally. "I just need to change my blouse. I don't want to get this one dirty."

She left to change her shirt and shortly returned to help.

I thought that would be all right and excused myself. Sally took my hand and started to lead me outside.

"It's good to have you back, son," said Bud.

"Yeah," added Patrick. "We'll start at the regular time in the morning. Supper will be at six tonight."

Sally, still holding my hand, led me down to the barn. When we got to the barn and before I could start unsaddling Roman, she wheeled me around and placed another big kiss on my lips. I was totally surprised!

"It's really good to have you back," she said, when she finished kissing. "You haven't kissed many girls, have you?"

This was beginning to sound familiar. I think I had heard it before, last summer when she kissed me goodbye.

"Ah … er … no," I said. "I didn't know where to go to learn an' get any practice. I better take care of my stock."

"You are really a shy, bashful country boy, aren't you?"

I wanted to say that I was just a plain simple cowboy, but I was feeling a little nervous in this conversation and wanting to change the subject. I broke loose from Sally's grip and turned to take the panniers off Matilda.

"What can I do to help?"

"You can take these canned goods up to the kitchen," I said. I couldn't believe I had wanted to see Sally so bad, and now I was sending her away.

"I'll be right back," she said, gathering up the cans.

By the time she returned, I'd unsaddled Roman and Matilda, and turned them out to pasture. All I had to do was take my bedroll and panniers to the bunkhouse. Sally took one pannier and I took the other and my bedroll and we headed to the bunkhouse. After unpacking the panniers and putting the clothes away, we took the panniers back to the barn.

"Your letters were welcome all winter, although they weren't really the love letters I expected," said Sally.

"Well, I'm not accustomed to being addressed as 'dumb' an' 'stupid' an' 'jerk'," I replied.

"I was just joking," she said. She was becoming a little somber. "I didn't realize you were so sensitive."

"I ain't really," I said, "an' you said your friends were surprised you had a boyfriend. I was surprised to hear that! You're good lookin' enough, you could have all the boyfriends you wanted, an' ..."

I was interrupted.

"I was referring to you, stupid! You're my boyfriend!"

"What?!" I was shocked.

"That's right! Didn't you know?"

"No," I said, still in shock.

"That's kind of dumb and stupid. Why do you think you got a letter once a week? And how were they all signed?"

"There you go with the dumb an' stupid," I said. I was surprised. "Why would you want a dumb an' stupid boyfriend anyway?"

"Then I can train him the way I want him," she replied. "Besides that, you can rope a little. You're almost as good as I am!"

Sally had an amused look on her face and I couldn't tell if she was serious or just pulling my leg. If she was serious, I had to make some sort of plan, to do just what, I didn't know. If she was joking, well the laugh was on me. Either way, I guess the joke was on me. I didn't know what to say.

"You really didn't know, did you?"

"I guess not," I said. "I really don't know what to do—I never had a girlfriend before." I let that slip out and didn't mean to. I was blushing again.

"I thought as much," said Sally. "I'll give you a few pointers. I thought that beautiful blouse you sent me for Christmas kinda sealed the deal."

"That was a Christmas gift," I said. "I'd hoped you'd like it."

"I love it and I won't wear it for anyone but you!"

I sure couldn't tell anyone that buying that shirt was a mistake and sending it to her was an afterthought. I was going to have to watch my words more carefully in the future. And my actions.

"I guess we ought to head up for supper," I said, not knowing what else to say.

"You don't like the idea of having a girlfriend?"

This girl could ask some of the most confusing questions.

"Well," I stammered and stuttered, "Ah … yes, I do. But I … ah … I never had a girlfriend before. I don't know, or … ah … I'm not sure what to do, or say."

"You just be yourself," she said, "your shy, bashful self. That's what I like about you!"

I started to say that I didn't think there was anything she liked about me, but decided to keep my mouth shut. Silence might be the best option at this point.

We headed up to the lodge for supper, with Sally holding my hand all the way. I felt like I was walking on air. I had a girlfriend! And I didn't have to do anything to get her! It was her idea! I was quite pleased with myself.

Supper was spent visiting with Bud, Pat, and the other hands, Jeff, Dave, and Jim. The cook was the same one that was here last year—he'd been here quite a few years. It was good to see him again and I knew there would be plenty of good eating all summer.

Sally sat right next to me, and kept the questions coming. I was doing most of the talking, a position I wasn't used to. I had to tell all how my Dad got the mountain lion, how Tommy and I didn't place at the rodeo in the team roping, and how I had to have my appendix out.

I finally asked Bud, "What's the overall plan for the summer? When do the dudes start gettin' here?"

"We've got a fairly full summer of dudes. They'll show up on

Sundays, stay a week, and leave the following Saturday morning. We have a few girls coming to do the maid work; one of them is a friend of Sally's from school. You'll have to take them out riding on occasion, when they and you have some free time. Then …"

"I'll be going on those rides also," interrupted Sally, as she gave her dad a disapproving look.

Bud laughed, along with Patrick. "Most assuredly," replied Bud, "most assuredly!"

Sally gave me a look of triumph.

Bud continued, "We'll do some branding about every two weeks, and take the dudes out to check the cattle almost every day. I've got some colts that can be started, and I want them all gentle so we can use them for the dudes when the time's ready. If the dudes are interested, they can come down to the round corral and watch you work the colts. Having a crowd around will be good for them."

"I want to start my own colt," said Sally. "He should be big enough to start riding now."

"As I recall," continued Bud, "last year you put on a roping clinic for the dudes and it went over pretty well. You can put on a horse breaking clinic for the dudes along with a roping clinic."

"I didn't see any broodmare bunches out here last year," I said.

"That reminds me," said Bud. "We need to run in the broodmare bunch and get the colts branded. I haven't seen any of them since I drove out there a month ago. We also need to run in the young horses so you can start playing with them. They've all been halter broke and they lead good. They've all had a lot of groundwork done on them. The broodmare bunch is up on the north end, all you saw last year was the south end.

"Lets see, today's Tuesday. Tomorrow, I need to go to town

and pick up Missus Abercrombie, she's going to spend the whole summer like she does every year. You remember her. She took quite a liking to you last year, even after you chewed her out about following one cow through the herd last summer. I also need to pick up the maids; they'll be coming on the bus.

"You fellers can gather the broodmare bunch tomorrow morning then bring in the young horses in the afternoon.

"The girls can get the cabins and rooms ready Wednesday and we'll brand the colts in the morning."

Pat shot Bud a disapproving look and Bud noticed it.

"No," said Bud, "I'll stay out of the way. I can't do much with this bum foot, anyways. The first guests arrive Sunday, so we'll have a few days to kinda relax and get to know everyone."

The Work Begins

The next morning, I caught Roman in the little holding pasture, saddled him, and helped jingle the horses in. I watched Jeff, Dave, and Jim ride as we brought the horses in at a run. It looked like to me that they weren't really good riders—they all had a good, stout hold on their saddle horns.

"That was fun," said Dave when we got to the corrals. "I don't think I've ever rode that fast before!"

I wondered what Bud was thinking when he hired these guys; they didn't appear to be cowboys or horsemen.

Sally helped bring in the horses and it was invigorating to watch her ride. The horse and her worked just like one unit together. I figured she could ride anything on the ranch and she rode a lot better than the other three fellers.

"You can use him or saddle Drygulch," Pat said to me. "I've already ridden him this year. We'll have plenty of work for either one of them today. If you use Drygulch, keep your horse in a pen this morning. We'll turn him out with the saddle horses tonight. Your donkey should be all right in that holding pasture for now."

That was Pat's way of letting me know that Drygulch should

be all right. He'd been ridden already this year and probably wouldn't buck. It's interesting how people with the same backgrounds can communicate without coming out with a long, lengthy dialogue. I knew exactly what Pat meant.

"I'll use Drygulch," I said. "My horse has been used every day for the last week; a little rest won't hurt him." Pat knew exactly what I meant, wanting to give my personal horse a rest.

I'd ridden Drygulch the summer before and he was a good horse. I thought he was a little faster than Roman and thought I might need the extra speed bringing in the broodmare bunch.

Sally rode right next to me and the three other hands followed us. I hadn't noticed until after we started out, but Pat had replaced his lariat rope with a bullwhip. I wondered what that was for, but didn't say anything.

As we headed for the north part of the ranch, Pat told me how the country laid and the way the horses were liable to run when we started them.

"We'll try to get a count on them before they start. If we don't, that's all right, that old stud keeps a pretty close watch on his harem. Keep an eye on him, he's broke an' don't have much respect for riders. In the corral, you can halter him and lead him around, but you still got to watch him. He's all stud. Are you guys listening? Keep an eye on the stud! He'll take you an' your horse if he gets a chance!"

We located the bunch about six or seven miles from the ranch. The stud was off to one side grazing. One of the broodmares noticed us first and let out a snort. The paint stud instantly became alert and started out to meet us.

"You boys get behind the mares an' colts an' start them toward the ranch. Sally, you make sure they get 'em goin' right. You come with me; we'll teach that ol' stud a lesson."

67

I followed Pat while the others made a circle around the broodmares. We headed straight for the big paint stud as he came out to meet us.

"Come up here ahead of me," said Pat, as he took down the bullwhip. "If that stud wants to chase you, let him. I'll slip in behind him an' teach him a lesson or two. Don't be afraid to let Drygulch out, you might have to."

I wasn't sure what was happening, but did as I was told.

The stud approached us and from the way his ears were laid back against his neck, I could tell this was not going to be a social call.

"Better start runnin' an' do it fast!" hollered Pat. "I'll be right behind both of you."

I kicked Drygulch into a fast run as the stud took out after us. He was almost close enough that he could bite Drygulch. I urged Drygulch on and he was going as fast as he could. We kept it up for a couple of hundred yards.

I was beginning to wonder if Drygulch was fast enough to keep out of reach of the stud when I heard the crack of Pat's bullwhip. I looked back as I heard the crack again.

The stud slowed a little and the whip cracked again. A couple of more cracks and the stud abandoned his chase of me and began to look for his mares.

"I think we taught him a lesson," said Pat, as we slowed our horses to a trot and followed a couple of hundred yards behind him. "I hope the boys give him plenty of room when he gets to the mares. He could be trouble for them. Sally will probably warn them. She's pretty smart."

"You have some interesting teaching methods," I said.

"Yep, it generally works. A few buttonholes out of his hide

will make him think twice about coming out and greeting people the way he does."

"I didn't know you meant you'd be behind me an' the stud. I thought you meant you'd be behind me an' Drygulch," I said.

Pat laughed.

"You're pretty handy with that whip," I said.

"Yeah," said Pat. "Put a smoke in your mouth an' I'll show you just how handy I really am! I'll cut it right in half." He let out a good laugh.

"I don't smoke," I said. "It doesn't look like you really needed me to gather the horses."

"Yes, I needed you. I couldn't have done it without you. The new hands can't ride good enough to do what we did, an' I certainly didn't want to use Sally."

"What you really mean is you needed someone to be the bait," I said.

"Well, sort of."

"Why didn't you tell me what you had in mind?"

"You might not have wanted to do it," replied Pat, grinning. "We better catch up an' see how things are goin'."

The stud had caught up to his mares and Sally had the hands well behind the horses. The lead mare was headed the right direction and Pat and I fell in behind the other riders.

Sally asked, "What did you do?"

"We went fishin'," answered Pat.

"Yeah, with me as bait," I said.

"We just needed to teach that stud a lesson," said Pat. "Did anybody get a count on the mares?"

"They're all there," said Sally. "I recognized all of them. And the colts look real good! I don't know which one I want!"

"They should all be good," said Pat, "that stud has some pretty powerful bloodlines. That's why your dad got him."

We got the broodmare band in the corral without further incident.

Pat told me, "Get a rope on the stud an' I'll get a halter on him. We need to separate him from the mares an' colts. Sally, go get your dad. He'll want to look over his colt crop."

"Dad's already headed here," said Sally. "You couldn't keep him away when the mares show up."

I saw Bud hobbling toward the corral from the lodge. He had something in his hand but I couldn't see what it was.

I got a rope on the stud and he didn't hit the end of it hard. When it settled around his neck, he just stopped and snorted. He'd been handled before.

Pat slipped up the rope, put the halter on and led the stud to another pen.

"Jeff, Dave, and Jim," said Bud, "get the pickup and bring about thirty bales of hay up from the lower ranch. It's right there in the stack yard. Turn your horses loose first.

"Daughter," he said to Sally, "how do you like the looks of that colt crop?"

"They all look good to me," said Sally. "And they're all spotted!"

"We are in the paint horse business," said Bud, "they're supposed to be spotted. Get some halters from the barn. We'll catch the mares and tie them up, and then we can better tell what colt belongs to what mare."

Sally and I went to the barn to get the halters. As we left I saw Bud hobble over to the stud and start talking to him, like they were old friends. Pat was nearby, putting some salve on the buttonholes he had cut out of the stud's rump with the bullwhip.

70

We returned with the halters and started to catch the mares. They were all halter broke and most of them had been ridden, but some were a little spooky, not having been handled for a year or so.

When they were all caught and tied to the fence, Bud, Pat, Sally, and I sat on the fence to look at the colts.

As we waited for things to settle down, Bud said to me, "I understand you had a good ride, young man."

"Yes sir," I said. "It was sorta fun. But I didn't know Pat was going to use me as bait!"

"He told me last night what he had in mind. I wish I could have been there and seen it!"

"I think you would have enjoyed it," I said.

"He's pretty good bait," said Pat.

Sally was busy looking over the colt crop. "Do you think that one will straighten up?"

She was pointing at a black and white colt that was pretty crooked in his front legs. A lot of colts are born with fairly crooked legs, as their environment before birth is cramped for as long as their legs are. Most of them straighten up as they grow up and a lot of those that don't can be helped with corrective shoeing.

"Probably, time will tell," answered Bud.

"We'll need to get a picture of each colt," said Bud. "But we can do that later."

I asked, "What do you need pictures for?"

"We need pictures for registration purposes," said Bud. "Those are all registered paint horses."

I wasn't familiar with registered horses. But I knew that there was quite a monetary investment in this bunch of broodmares. And the stud had to be registered, too.

Sally eased up to me. "Which one would you pick?"

"I don't know," I said. "There's a lot of growing to be done with all of them before I could make a sound choice."

"That makes sense," said Pat. "But the best one is that one over there."

He pointed to a sorrel and white colt standing with her mother.

"You only say that because that's your own mare and colt," said Sally.

Bud laughed. "That's a good colt and really wild colored! Get the Polaroid camera and take the pictures. I've got to get to town and pick up Missus Abercrombie and the new maids. What's the name of your friend, Sally?"

"Linda," replied Sally.

"I knew you couldn't go to town 'till you'd seen the colts," said Pat.

"I've still got plenty of time to get to town," said Bud, "but I better get going or I'll be out of time."

As Bud left, Sally said to me, "You'll like Linda, but not too much, I hope. I'll get the camera."

There were eighteen mares and all had colts by their sides. It was a fine looking colt crop.

The pictures were taken, one of each side of every colt. Pat did the picture taking, and Sally made notes regarding the mother of each colt. When the pictures of each colt were taken, I took the mare and her colt to the holding pasture and turned them loose with Matilda.

When the picture taking was done, we went to the lodge for a cup of coffee and discussed the colt crop. Sally was plainly excited. Presently, Jeff, Dave, and Jim showed up with a pickup load of hay. We unloaded the hay, except for six bales, then had our noon meal.

After eating, Sally, Pat, and I got our horses and went to another pasture to run in the young horses. These were two year olds and yearlings. I looked over these young horses real close, some of these were the colts I was going to start this summer.

There were twenty-one colts all totaled. There were only five two year olds in the bunch, the other colts being yearlings. All the yearlings were spotted. There weren't any spotted colts in the two year olds, but there were three buckskins, one grulla, and one bay colt. Two of the buckskins were line-backed buckskins and the other one was a canella buckskin—a red-colored dun.

"How come there ain't no paints in the two year olds?" I was curious.

"Dad's only had the paint stud for two years," said Sally. "The yearlings are his first crop of colts. They look good, don't they?"

"Yes," I said. "The two year olds are mostly buckskins, how come?"

"The old stud we had was an old remount stud and he threw mostly buckskin colts. One year we had fourteen buckskins and two grullas."

"What's a grulla?" Jeff and the other hands had showed up to watch.

"A grulla is a mouse-colored dun," replied Sally.

It occurred to me that these three hands were quite ignorant in the ways of a ranch. I wondered why Bud had hired them.

The colts were all caught and tied to the fence. Pat had taken time during the previous winters to halter break them and he had done a lot of groundwork with them. We all got brushes and curry combs and started to brush them, cleaning the winter hair that hadn't slicked off.

"They've all been worked quite a bit," said Pat. "You should be able to get on an' just ride off."

Pat had a grin on his face as he said that, and I wondered just exactly what he meant.

"You said you had a colt here," I said to Sally, "which one is it?"

"It's this one, the one I'm brushing," said Sally. She was brushing the grulla colt. "Isn't he beautiful?"

The colt did look nice, a grulla with four white stockings on his feet and a wide blaze down his nose. The white on his hind feet went up past his hocks and it made a striking picture.

"What do you call him?"

"I haven't really officially named him yet. I've been calling him 'Beauty.' What do you think?"

"I don't know," I said. "He is a nice lookin' horse."

The horse was nice looking and his coloring and markings indicated he would bring top dollar at a sale. I knew that I would need to do an extra special job breaking this horse for Sally.

As we brushed the horses, I asked everyone to pick up their horse's feet. As they did this, I watched. None of the colts objected to this. Pat had done a good job doing the groundwork.

"We did a lot of groundwork on these colts," said Pat. "All of them have had their feet picked up an' they've all been saddled with a kid's saddle when they were weaners! It shouldn't take much to get on an' start teachin' them to turn an' stop."

It was obvious Pat was proud of his work.

"It looks like you've done a good job," I said, trying to give Pat a real mature compliment.

"We'll play with these colts for a day or two, just to see what they remember, then get down to working with them," said Pat.

We brushed the colts for the better part of the afternoon, then scattered the six bales of hay we had left on the truck in the corral for their evening meal and called it a day.

"Bud will want to see the yearlings before we turn them back out," said Pat. "We'll keep 'em in overnight an' take 'em back to their pasture in the morning. Tomorrow, we'll put the two year olds in with the saddle horses. After we brand the colts, we'll take the broodmare bunch back to their pasture and turn 'em loose. We probably won't see 'em until fall, but they'll be all right. We don't want to take any dudes close to that broodmare bunch with that stud. Even though we gave him a lesson, he might be too dangerous to have them novice riders an' kids around."

Right before supper, Bud showed up with Missus Abercrombie and the girls that were to be the maids. Introductions were made all around. There was Linda, Sally's friend from school, a girl named Marie, and a girl named Josie. All three girls were really good looking, but I didn't think any of them were better looking than Sally.

Linda was a tall stately blonde and carried herself that way. Josie was a dishwater blonde, not quite as tall as Linda. Marie was shorter, with dark hair and dark eyes. Her eyes were intriguing, full of expression. I decided that Marie was the best looking of the three—after Sally, of course.

Missus Abercrombie remembered me from last year.

"The quiet boy that speaks his mind, bluntly," she said as she gave me a hug. "You keep it up."

I returned the hug.

"It's nice to see you again," I said. "You're looking well."

"Ah," she said, "you've learned how to stretch the truth!"

Everyone laughed at her comment. I could feel myself starting to blush.

Sally and Linda were busy catching up on the gossip they'd missed during the last week or ten days. The other two girls looked strangely uncomfortable and were quiet.

Trying to make the girls feel at ease, I asked them, "So where are you girls from?"

They looked at each other, not wanting to be the first one to speak, and then they both spoke at the same time.

"I'm from Iowa."

"I'm from New Hampshire."

They settled down and I said, "Now let's see you're Marie an' you're from Iowa an' you're …"

I was interrupted. "No, I'm Josie and I'm from Iowa and she's Marie and she's from New Hampshire."

"It might take me awhile to get you girls straight. But it don't make no difference where you're from, you're here now."

The girls giggled.

"What do you do for a living?"

"We're going to be maids. We still go to school," said Josie.

"Can you make a livin' goin' to school? I never could," I said.

They giggled some more.

Jeff, Dave, and Jim were just standing by, not doing anything.

"Here guys, grab these suitcases an' we'll take these girls inside," I said. "Sally, where are these girls goin' to live? I don't think we'll put 'em up in the barn, will we?"

The girls giggled again and Sally, looking somewhat surprised at my assertiveness, said, "Follow me."

The boys had picked up the girls' suitcases and followed

Sally to the girls' quarters. All that was left was Missus Abercrombie's bag.

"You travel pretty light," I said.

"I left most of my ranch clothes here last year," she said. "I come out here every year, been doing it for years. I can find my own room."

"I know that," I said, "but I thought you might protect me from those other girls!" I was trying to be funny.

"Sally will do that. She wrote to me about you quite often last winter."

"Oh? I hope she said something good."

"Don't you worry about it young man! Don't you worry!" Her reply was quite adamant. "Here's my room."

I set the bag at the door and turned to leave.

"You treat her nice. She's special!"

"Certainly," I said.

I left Missus Abercrombie, thinking about what she had just said. Sally had written to her about me. Was I a topic of gossip between them? I wondered.

Supper was fairly quiet that night. The girls didn't have much to say and only spoke when directly questioned. I didn't know it then, but that would change. Linda and Sally had a running dialogue and Bud and Missus Abercrombie discussed old times.

Before we left the table, Bud said, "We'll brand the colts in the morning then take the broodmare bunch back to their pasture. Sally, while we're doing that, you can take the girls and start getting the rooms ready. As usual, you'll be in charge of training the girls in their duties."

"I can help with that," said Missus Abercrombie. "I've helped with that for years."

"And we appreciate it," said Bud. "Any questions?"

Josie asked, "Where do we get the cleaning supplies, clean linen, and such?"

"Sally will show all of that to you in the morning. Breakfast is at six in the morning, don't be late," said Bud. "Get a good night's sleep tonight, tomorrow will be pretty busy!"

As we got up from the table, Sally grabbed my hand and quietly said, "Come with me."

She led me down toward the barn.

"I hope you don't think I was ignoring you. I haven't seen Linda since school let out and we had a lot to talk about."

"No," I said, thinking to myself, *I wonder what would happen if they hadn't seen each other for a year rather than a week or ten days?*

Inside the barn, Sally said, "Now we can practice."

"Practice what?"

"Kissing, stupid!"

"Oh! Well, to tell you the truth, I, ah … well, I don't really, ah …"

"You don't really know what you're doing," she said.

"That's right," I admitted.

"You don't have to tell me," she said. "First of all, you don't have to pucker up like you're kissing your mom. Just part your lips slightly, then put them gently on mine. Like this."

She proceeded to demonstrate—on me.

When she was done, I asked her, "How do you breathe?"

"Through your nose! This is going to take longer than I expected!"

We practiced for about twenty minutes, then decided to adjourn for the night. I walked her to the lodge, with her holding my hand all the way. It was sorta comfortable. We were to practice every night all summer long. At the lodge, I gave her a little kiss on the forehead, said goodnight and went to the bunkhouse.

Jeff, Dave, and Jim were still up, talking about the new arrivals. One of them asked, "What do you think of the new girls?"

"All three of 'em's pretty cute," I said. I really didn't want to divulge that I was already infatuated with Sally. I didn't pay much attention to them as I got ready for bed and they discussed the girls. It wasn't long before I was asleep.

A New Name

The next morning I was up early, before the boys were fully awake.

Pat and I saddled our horses to gather the saddle horses and as we saddled, Pat said, "This will be an interesting summer. The boys can't really ride and they've already shown a lot of interest in the new girls. The one boy can't ride at all. It's a wonder he didn't fall off yesterday."

"I noticed that," I said. "Why did Bud hire the boys anyway?"

"There's a reason. You'll find out later, I reckon. I tried to talk him out of it, but he wanted to give it a try. We'll see how it works out. Regardless, it's goin' to mean a lot more work for you an' me. You up to it?"

"I suppose so," I said.

"You'll probably need more than one horse during the summer. You can use your saddle horse or Drygulch or anything else you want except Bud's big paint horse an' my private saddle horse, this one I'm a ridin'."

"I've liked the looks of that big paint horse of Bud's ever since I first saw him. But nobody rides him but Bud, huh?"

"That's right."

Before we found the horses, Sally caught up to us.

"Thought you'd leave without me and have all the fun to yourselves, huh?" Sally was smiling as she said that.

"Yep, that was the idea," said Pat grinning.

"You can't get rid of me that easy," she said.

We found the horses shortly after Sally showed up. Pat got a quick count on them.

"Let's take 'em in," he said. He let out a war cry, Sally joined him and we were off. It was always exciting to chase the horses in at full speed. And it looked pretty neat, the horses running with manes and tails flying. It was invigorating.

Presently, the horses were corralled. We left our horses saddled in the corral.

"You go up an' get breakfast," said Pat, "I'll be up shortly. Check on the boys an' make sure they're up. I think they have a tendency to sleep in a little."

"I'll check on the girls," said Sally, "they might be the same way."

"I was goin' to do that," I said.

Sally gave me a dirty look, but smiled. "I can do it," she said.

The boys were up and we walked up to get breakfast, where we were joined by the girls. Jim had a noticeable limp.

I asked him, "Got a little hitch in your git-along?"

"Yeah," he said, sourly. "I'm sore! I might not be able to work today."

"Not used to ridin'? Better talk to Bud about not workin'," I said.

Bud was already at the table, sipping his coffee.

Shortly, Pat joined us. "He's okay," said Pat.

Bud gave him a knowing look and said, "Daughter, today

after we get the colts branded and you get the girls lined out, I want you to help take the broodmare bunch back to their pasture."

I could see the obvious pleasure on Sally's face. It replaced the disappointment she showed in not being able to help with the branding.

"And," he continued, "I want you to ride my big paint gelding."

The squeal of delight was very vocal coming from Sally.

"I won't be able to use him for a while and I don't want him going sour on me," concluded Bud.

"I already saddled him for you. He's ready when you are," said Pat.

Now I knew why Pat had stayed behind. He had topped off Bud's horse for Sally.

I immediately felt a little resentful and a little jealous. If I was Sally's boyfriend, I should be topping off her horses and protecting her. After all, I thought I was a pretty fair bronc rider to boot. Besides, I was told nobody but Bud rode that horse.

We started to the corral. Sally stayed behind and I saw her talking with Bud and Jim.

Sally came down to the corral. "Jim won't be helping you guys," she said. "He's going to help with the housekeeping, laundry, and in the kitchen. He says he's not a cowboy, and doesn't want to be one. But with him working housekeeping, I'll be able to work more with you and the horses and cattle."

She looked at me, smiling. I was pleased.

Pat said, "He hasn't been here a day an' already wants to work with the girls. I knew we should have hired another feller like you, a guy that ain't got no interest in girls."

He looked at me, with a quizzical smile on his face.

Sally looked at me and said, "That's not exactly true, is it Honey?"

I started … what??

Pat, Jeff, and Dave were laughing.

Honey? Things were happening around here faster than I was used to. I felt my face turning a little red.

Trying to diffuse the situation and divert the attention from me, I said, "He told me this mornin' he was pretty sore after ridin' yesterday. He couldn't hardly walk into breakfast."

"He was all over that saddle yesterday," said Pat.

Sally said, "I have to get back and start showing the housekeeping crew what to do. Don't take the broodmare bunch back until I can help you. I'll be down after the noon meal."

"Yeah," said Pat. "We better get to work. Get your horse, Honey, an' we'll run in the broodmare bunch."

I shot Pat a dirty look with the reference to "Honey," but he had a big broad grin on his face. I knew he was just kidding me, but it was embarrassing.

"You boys feed the colts in that corral an' just wait in the barn 'till we get the horses in. We won't be long." Pat gave a few more instructions to Jeff and Dave and we were off to gather the broodmare bunch.

"You topped off Bud's horse for Sally this morning?"

"Yeah," said Pat.

"I kinda thought I was goin' do the rough stock ridin'," I said. I didn't want to come right out and say that as Sally's boyfriend, I should be doing that sort stuff for her.

"Well, Honey," said Pat, still kidding me, "you'll get plenty of that when you start ridin' the colts. But Bud's horse hasn't been used since Bud got busted up an' he can be a little tough when he's not used regularly."

We found the broodmare bunch and started them toward the corral. I noticed that Matilda had joined the broodmare bunch. I took the lead and set out on a good trot. I could hear the pop of Pat's whip behind me and figured Pat was adding to the stud's education.

When we had the horses corralled, Pat haltered the stud and tied him in another corral. I caught Matilda and tied her outside the corral.

We started a fire and put the irons in.

"You rope the colts, Honey," said Pat. "Don't let 'em hit the end of the rope hard, be real easy on 'em. I'll slip up the rope, blindfold 'em an' we'll hit 'em with the iron. If we have to, we can use the gate as a chute, an' the boys can help hold 'em still."

I got the instructions, but bristled at the reference to "Honey." If I was going to have a nickname, I'd have sure picked something different.

The irons were hot. "Catch a colt," said Pat.

I roped a colt without letting him hit the end of the rope hard and Pat slipped up the rope and blindfolded him. Bud had hobbled down to the corral to watch, but stayed out of the corral. The boys helped out, trying to keep the colts still while they were branded.

The branding went well, and I was a little surprised at how well the blindfold worked, although Jeff was kicked a couple of times. He just shook it off and kept working.

Soon we were done.

"That will bring all the colts home," said Bud. "Let's get a cup of coffee and some lunch while we're waiting for Sally to get done. She'll be madder than all get out if you leave without her."

I got the impression that in the past, some colts didn't come home, that they had been stolen.

Pat said, "That sounds like a good idea, doesn't it Honey?"

"Yeah." I could feel my face getting red again and it wasn't from the sun.

"Honey!" Bud had heard Pat. "What's this Honey?" Bud was grinning, he already knew.

"It's his new nickname," said Pat.

I coiled my rope and strapped it on my saddle not saying a word. But I could feel my face flushing.

Sally joined us after she had shown the housekeeping crew what to do.

"How is Jim working out?" I was a little jealous that Sally was going to have a boy working on her crew.

"He's kinda stiff. I guess his riding yesterday was too much for him. But he does seem willing. He should be all right as soon as he works out the stiffness. Let's go move the broodmares! I can't wait to ride Dad's horse!"

We finished our coffee and the noon meal and started toward the barn.

"What do you want to do with her?" Pointing toward Matilda, Bud continued, "You can leave her with the broodmare bunch or keep her in close with the saddle horses. If you leave her with the mares, she might come in pregnant."

"She might already be," said Pat.

"Let's keep her in close," said Sally. "I have an idea on how we can use her during the summer."

"It makes no difference to me." I said. We put Matilda in the corral with the saddle horses.

Sally and I took the lead, setting the pace at a stiff trot. Bud's horse was ready to go, but Sally didn't have any trouble settling him down. *She sure can ride,* I thought as I watched her.

Occasionally, we heard the sound of Pat's bullwhip behind

us. I kept looking back to see if he needed some help, but he appeared to have everything under control. When we reached the pasture where the mares belonged, Sally and I peeled off, making sure we had plenty of room in case the stud wanted to challenge us. The mares filed past us, picking up speed as they went. They knew where they were going.

I think our horses appreciated the rest. We had set a good pace coming out to the pasture. Pat arrived and coiled his whip in his saddle.

"That's the last we'll see of them 'till fall," he said. "They'll be all right."

We rode slowly back to the ranch. I was anxious to get back and start working the two-year-old colts. Sally's horse had settled down some and it was a pleasant ride. We spent the time talking about the upcoming summer and what we could expect.

When we arrived at the ranch, Sally left immediately after unsaddling her horse to see how the housekeeping crew was doing. Jeff, Dave, and I caught up the two year olds and started brushing them.

"We'll get some saddles from the barn that aren't being used and I'll saddle these guys. We'll let them stand awhile and re-member, then lead them around some."

Presently, Sally showed up and began brushing her grulla colt. She talked to him in very soothing terms, almost like she talked to me when we were alone. I almost felt a little jealous as I listened to her.

Jealous of a horse? Ridiculous, I thought to myself. I felt kinda foolish, but still a little jealous.

Later, we saddled the colts. Pat had done a good job doing the groundwork; none of them raised a fuss while being saddled. They remembered.

I was anxious to get on and start riding them, but decided not to rush things. The more time a feller takes with young horses, generally the better the result. The afternoon was spent fiddling with the colts.

At the end of the day, we unsaddled the colts and turned them in to the saddle horse pasture and turned the saddle horses loose. We kept in two horses for Pat and me to jingle the horses in.

"You only kept two horses in," said Dave. "What will I ride to help you in the morning?"

"If you want to help in the morning," said Pat, "you'll have to get up earlier. We'll keep a horse in for you day after tomorrow if you want to go. An' we'll have to keep in a horse for Sally."

The next couple of days were spent playing with the colts and getting ready for the arrival of the dudes. Bud spent a lot of time at the corrals, obviously irritated that he couldn't do much.

Dave helped jingle the horses in each morning. His riding was getting better, but he had a long way to go before he felt comfortable enough in the saddle to let go of the saddle horn. Sally helped, and I began to wonder if Dave's helping out was just an excuse to be close to her.

The Bronc Stomper

After a couple of days playing on the ground with the colts, the time came to get on them and start riding. I'd already put a foot in the stirrup and eased myself up on each one of them, but hadn't got on all the way. Today would be the day, and I was excited.

I'd broke some horses for my dad, but we'd sold most of them as started ranch horses. Dad still had a few of the horses I'd started, and they were good ranch horses.

"Don't get on Beauty," said Sally. "I want to be the first one on him and the only one to ever ride him."

I started on the other colts first. Pat offered to snub the colts while I got on, but I didn't think it was necessary. They had stood well while I had eased myself up.

Bud came down to the corral to watch. "There could be a rodeo," he said. Jeff and Dave were on hand, just watching.

"You boys can unsaddle the colts when he's done with 'em, then turn 'em out with the saddle horses."

I got on each colt and rode them for about fifteen or twenty minutes in the round corral. They stood well while I got on, only moving to adjust to the added weight as I eased into the saddle. I didn't have any problem with any of them, although they really didn't know what to do when I pulled their heads around and asked them to move. I started them with a hackamore. I wanted to be easy on their mouths, so they'd respond better when we bitted them up.

I left the grulla colt for Sally. Soon she showed up and wanted to start her colt.

"Are you sure you don't want me to get on him first? This is all new to him, there's no tellin' what he'll do," I said.

"He'll be all right," said Sally. "Besides, I think he likes me!"

I couldn't speak for the horse, I thought, *but I knew I sure did.*

Pat insisted he snub the colt for Sally. "It's for your own safety. This colt has shown a little more fight than the others." With Pat snubbing the horse, Sally put her foot in the stirrup and eased into the saddle. The colt humped up a little and moved forward, but he couldn't do much as Pat had him pretty tight.

When he settled down, Pat said, "Rock back and forth in the saddle a little to get him used to it. He'll be all right. Then we'll move out. I'll lead him around a little. Just nudge him a little to get him goin'."

"But I don't want him to be a follower," said Sally.

"He won't be," replied Pat. "I'll play out a little rope as we move around. He'll be going on his own."

Sally nudged the colt a little in the sides and the colt jumped forward again. He couldn't go far or do much, Pat had him snubbed close.

"I told you he had more in him than the others!"

They moved around the corral easily and slowly eased into a trot. The colt took a jump as they moved into the trot and I could see a look of concern on her face.

"You're all right," said Pat. "Just keep goin'."

"But I don't want him to buck!" Sally's voice had a note of concern in it and I supposed it was more for the horse than her own welfare.

"I've got his lead," said Pat. "He won't buck ... hard."

They rode around the corral for about twenty minutes at a slow jog trot.

"He's really smooth going," said Sally. "He'll be fun and easy to ride when he grows up!"

When she was done riding, Dave offered to unsaddle the colt, but Sally refused. "This is my horse, I'll take care of him and my saddle."

I admired Sally's attitude, taking care of her own stuff. But I wondered if Dave was ahead of me in the social graces by volunteering to help her. I decided to ask her later that night when we had our kissing practice.

"This is yours," she said, handing me the hackamore.

"I've got another one I'll bring down an' give to you," I said. "It doesn't have the mecate; it's got seven-foot leather reins. You can have it, I don't like it much, I like the soft cotton mecate I used today, and it's easier on the hands."

"I like that one, too!"

That settled it for me. I knew I would be getting Sally a hackamore with a soft cotton mecate for Christmas. There wouldn't be any passing off my mistakes as Christmas gifts in the future.

Sally said, "What's that look on your face? You look like a light bulb just went off in your head!"

"It did," I said.

We turned the saddle horses and the colts out for the night; our day's work was done. We started to the lodge.

"The dudes will be showing up soon. I'll check with Bud an'

we'll see what the schedule is. I want to take the colts outside the corral but don't want a big crowd around when I do. After they've had a day or two to think about it, they might object an' take to bucking a little," I said.

"That sounds good to me," said Pat. He was letting me take charge of the horse breaking and I assumed he approved of what I was doing. However, he was still keeping Sally and her horse on a lead and giving her some pointers as she moved along breaking her horse. The grulla had offered to buck more than once, but Pat had kept him in close and didn't let him get started.

I felt a little jealous about Pat helping Sally. She was my girl-friend and I should be helping her. I felt kinda silly; I was jealous of Pat, Jim, Dave, and a horse where this girl was concerned. *There's a lot of jealousy when a feller has a girlfriend,* I thought. I pushed the jealousy thoughts aside—I had work to do and couldn't be sidetracked with such thoughts.

If I get up the nerve, I'll discuss it with her during our kissing practice one of these nights, I thought. Our practice sessions had become a nightly occurrence, and I looked forward to them. I thought I was getting better.

I discussed the situation with Bud. He agreed that it might not be a good idea to ride the colts outside the corral with the dudes too soon.

"You can help with the dudes in the morning, and then work the colts in the afternoon."

The dudes had arrived and the leisurely pace that we had enjoyed previously vanished. The main emphasis was toward the dudes and their welfare. The saddle horses were still gathered at the same time each day, and the horses we expected to use were saddled right after breakfast.

Bud came down to the corrals each morning to watch the

91

procedures. There wasn't much need for supervising, Pat and I both knew what to do. Jeff and Dave needed a little extra help; they had a hard time learning the horses and their names. Bud was helpful with the boys and very patient. I knew where Sally's patience with me came from. Bud was mostly interested in how Sally was doing with her horse and she would arrive after she had completed her head housekeeping duties.

I was amazed; she could do it all.

The next day, I saddled one of the line-backed buckskins right after breakfast. Pat and Jeff and Dave were going to take the dudes on a leisurely ride and I wasn't needed. I was going to take all four of the colts and ride them outside the round pen. Sally showed up and saddled the big paint horse her dad rode.

"Dad thought it might be a good idea if I went with you this morning," she said. "Is that all right with you, Honey?"

It was more than all right with me, although I bristled at the "Honey" nickname."

"What about your housekeeping duties?"

"They'll be all right. You know, Jim's really taken charge of the girls and I'm thinking of making him head housekeeper. He does a really good job!"

I felt myself becoming a little more jealous of Jim.

"That will give me more of an opportunity to come down here to the corrals and help you guys. I'd rather be down here anyways," she said, smiling. I wondered if she knew that I was thinking the same thing.

I didn't say anything, but thought to myself, *I'd rather have you down here anyways too!*

As soon as Sally saddled the paint, I got on the buckskin. I rode him around the corral a little, just to make sure he hadn't forgotten what he'd already learned about turning and stopping. Things went well.

"Open the gate," I said. "I'm gettin' tired of ridin' in the corral."

Sally opened the gate. I waited for her to get mounted and we started out. We rode through the saddle horse pasture. The colt moved easily and I didn't really expect any trouble from him. He even crossed the little creek that ran through the pasture without a fuss. We rode for about an hour all totaled by the time we returned to the corral.

Sally and I just talked the whole time. It was very pleasant.

I unsaddled the colt and caught the canella buckskin and got him ready to go outside the corral. The procedure was the same as it was with the first colt, although I thought this colt might give me some problems. He'd resisted his training more than the other colts.

When we reached the creek, the colt balked at going into the water.

"Go through the creek first, Sally. This guy's a little scared of the water."

Sally went through the creek, but the colt refused. I spurred him a little more aggressively, but he still refused.

"Come, go through it again, Sally, an' watch out, I'll be right behind you!"

I took the mecate from my belt and prepared to give this colt a little stronger encouragement, right over his rump.

Sally came across the creek and started back across. I spurred the colt harder and gave him a hard whack over his rump with the end of my mecate. That brought results!

The surprised colt jumped the creek, almost bumping into Sally and the paint. The paint horse spooked a little, but Sally kept him under control. Much to my surprise, the colt took another jump! If he was going to buck, this would be the time for it.

He took another jump and I heard Sally yelling, "Ride him cowboy! Stay with him, Honey!"

I pulled his head up and he stopped bucking.

"Let's do that again," I said.

"You really like riding bucking horses, don't you?"

"That's not the point," I said. "This here colt is a little scared of the water an' I aim to teach him that there ain't nothin' to be scared of."

We crossed the creek again. The colt jumped it again, but he didn't come across bucking. We repeated the procedure a few more times until the colt decided to stop jumping the creek and get his feet wet. The last time we crossed, I had Sally follow me. The colt was crossing the creek and doing it willingly.

"We'll have to come back an' repeat this for a couple of days," I said. "I don't want him to forget this lesson."

We rode back to the corral and I saddled the other linebacked buckskin. The procedure was the same once again. At the creek, the colt hesitated, but walked through the water. The rest of the ride was uneventful.

I saddled the bay colt when we got back to the corral. I didn't think there would be any problem with this horse and there wasn't. We made the same ride.

During each ride out of the corral, I was regularly turning the colts around trees and sagebrush to teach them to turn better. I used a short pulling motion on the hackamore, rather than a steady pull when I wanted to go around an object. If I wanted to go right, I would tug on the right mecate and lay the left mecate on the left side of the colt's neck. I was teaching them to neck rein as we went along.

When we returned to the corral, Pat and the boys had returned with the dudes. The dudes were all excited—they had seen some deer.

"I think," said Sally, "I want to take Beauty outside the corral. He's ready for it."

"Let's do that after dinner," said Pat.

I was sure he wanted to check with Bud and make sure it was all right before he agreed to the idea.

After the noon meal, Sally saddled the grulla. The colt had acted more respectful with more handling, and Pat wasn't snubbing the horse any more when Sally got on.

Sally got on the colt, rode him around the corral a few times and was ready to go out of the corral. Pat opened the gate. I'd saddled Roman and rode along with them, watching the grulla closely. I didn't really trust the colt a hundred percent yet.

The ride was uneventful until we got to the creek. The colt balked.

"I'll start across first," said Pat. "Maybe he'll follow my horse."

"I can crowd him from the rear, if you want," I said.

The horse still didn't want to cross, so Sally urged him a little more forcefully with the spur. It didn't take much. The colt bogged his head, snorted and bucked across the creek. The colt didn't stop bucking when he got across; he kept it up, getting a little more strength and enthusiasm with each jump.

Sally was trying to pull his head up. She had a hand on each rein, but she didn't have the strength and with each jump, she was loosening up in the saddle.

Pat was hollering, "Hold on! Hold on!" He'd turned his horse around and was on the left side of the grulla.

I spurred Roman into a run and came up along side the colt's right side. I was yelling, "Pull his head up! Pull his head up!"

Pat and I had the horse more or less cornered—all he could do was buck straight. But he was doing a good job of that.

I changed my reins from my left hand to my right hand and put my left arm around Sally's waist. Pat had got the left rein and jerked the colt's head up and dallied up.

"Clear your stirrups," I said. "We'll get you off this critter. Put your arms around me."

Sally did as she was told, and I got her off the horse. I brought Roman to a stop and set Sally on the ground as gently as possible. Pat had gotten the grulla colt settled down, and wasn't far away.

"You don't ever have to tell me to put my arms around you," said Sally. "I can do that anytime, Honey!"

I could see that she was more than willing.

"Are you all right? That horse really came unglued," I said.

Pat came up a little closer. "That colt of yours ain't really a house pet, is he? Maybe you ought to let Honey here ride him back. I sorta think there's more of that in him."

"No," said Sally. "I rode him out here and I'll ride him back. This was just a little misunderstanding."

"Don't let him buck no more," I said. "He might decide he likes it and want to keep it up. Take a breather an' we'll try that again. I can ride him around some an' see if he's got it out of his system."

"Nope," said Sally.

We took a little rest, and then Sally was ready to get on again. Pat had snubbed up the colt and I eased up on the right side of the colt. The only way the colt could move was forward. Sally got on, took the rein Pat was snubbing the horse with and said, like nothing had happened, "Let's go."

We rode away from the creek, and I knew full well we'd have to cross it to get back to the ranch. But this time, we'd be better prepared.

The creek crossing on the way back didn't pose the problem we had the first time. The colt hesitated a little at the water, put his head down and followed Pat's horse across, like the good horse he was supposed to grow up to be.

Sally was full of praise and a lot of pats on the neck for the horse. "I wouldn't go to trustin' him too much," I said. "There's something about him that just ain't trustworthy at this point."

Pat nodded his head in silent agreement.

Sally asked, "Did he buck as hard as the red dun colt did this morning?"

"Did the red dun buck?" Pat hadn't been filled in as to what happened earlier in the day.

"He didn't really buck," I said. "He just crow hopped a little at the creek. I might have tried to push him across a little too fast."

"A feller has to be careful with these young horses around water," said Pat. "I'm told they don't have good depth perception an' can't really tell how deep the water is. He didn't buck you off did he, Honey?"

I bristled at the reference to "Honey." "Of course not. He didn't buck near as hard as Sally's horse did. You did a good job of ridin' him, Sally. Where and when did you become a bronc stomper?"

"I've rode a bucking horse or two," replied Sally.

"Mostly by accident," said Pat.

"I beg your pardon!" Sally said, sounding quite upset.

"Ah … I didn't, ah … mean that like it sounded," said Pat.

It was nice to see that Sally had Pat stammering and stuttering, although it was for different reasons than why she had me stammering and stuttering.

"What I meant was that you were on some horses you shouldn't have been on."

Pat was working himself out of this one quite nicely, I thought. I just watched and listened, thinking I might learn something.

"But I rode them!"

"True, true," replied Pat. He was willing to drop the matter.

I continued to ride the colts during the afternoons, the mornings being spent with the dudes. Sally would join me when she could, riding Bud's big paint horse. We were just riding around the country, pleasure riding. We did have destinations in mind. I started joining the dude rides on my colts, as they were coming along well, learning more about neck reining each day. Sally and Pat would take her grulla horse out in the afternoon.

I missed riding with Sally in the afternoon, but Sally and Pat kept me informed on the grulla's progress.

A Job for Matilda

We gathered a bunch of cattle and held a branding. The dudes tried roping, without much success. One of the dudes even caught a calf, but lost his rope. Sally roped the calf easily and we branded the calf and retrieved the rope.

Jeff and Dave did the groundwork, refusing to even try and rope a calf. I thought they were probably trying to avoid embarrassment to themselves. Pat and I switched around on the roping and the groundwork. Sally roped most of the time.

I enjoyed watching Sally rope. She was good. I was a little apprehensive when my turn came to rope; I sure didn't want to miss when she was watching. At least she wasn't keeping score, like my brother Tommy did.

Bud came to the branding, driving to the corrals in the truck. He had a big bucket of soda pop on ice and it really made a big hit with the dudes.

"I've got to get to town and get this cast off," said Bud. "You guys are having too much fun without me down here!"

That night, we held a square dance. I felt fully prepared, having had some lessons in our kitchen back home. I found out why Bud had hired Jeff, Dave, and Jim—they were the band! And they were good! Jeff could even call the square dances. Jeff played guitar, Dave played fiddle, and Jim played bass guitar.

I felt some pangs of jealousy again as I listened to them play, and they became stronger when Sally asked me, "You don't play any musical instruments, do you?"

"Oh, yes I do," I said.

"Really? What do you play?"

"I don't play well, but I can play it two ways," I said, not wanting to be out done.

Sally asked, "What is it?"

"It's my nose; I blow it and pick it!"

I got a disgusted look from Sally, but she was laughing.

"You're terrible," she said.

"Yeah, but you're laughing. Let's go dance," I said, reaching for her hand.

Sally looked surprised, "I guess you did learn something about social graces in social studies class. I thought you'd never ask me."

Actually, I had been waiting for her to ask me. I still wasn't a hundred percent comfortable in these social situations. Besides that, all the dudes were there and I wasn't sure just how to do it. But I had learned—just ask!

We strolled out to the dance floor to get ready for the next square dance. Mentally, I was preparing myself. I remembered my mother saying, "All you have to do to square dance is know your right from your left."

The dance started and I made it all the way through without making the wrong turn or bumping into anybody. When it was over, we went outside for a breather.

"Where did you learn to square dance?"

"I been thinkin' about it a lot," I replied.

"Well, who have you been practicing with?"

There was a tone of indignation in Sally's voice as she asked the question. *Was there a little hint of jealousy?* I wondered.

"My mother," I answered.

"Your mother! Are you sure?"

Now, I was sure there was some jealousy. It made me feel strangely good.

"Yep," I said. "Who else?"

Sally didn't say anything, but it seemed like she relaxed a little. We went back in and danced some more. The boys could play some two-step music and I really liked that; I could hold Sally close.

"Oops," I said as I stepped on her foot. "I'm sorry."

"Don't be sorry," said Sally. "You're a marvelous dancer. Did your mother teach you that, too?"

"Yep," I said. "Oops," I stepped on her foot again. Her thinking that I was a marvelous dancer would soon be downgraded to "good" dancer.

"My mother also told me that you'd learn to keep your feet out from under mine, just as she had to learn with my dad." I was trying to be reassuring to her.

"I wish she was here tonight to teach me," she whispered.

"What's that?" I'd heard just enough to make me think her comment was uncomplimentary.

"Oh, nothing," she replied.

We danced pretty well into the night. I hadn't paid much attention to the time, but it was getting kinda late. Pat had already left, probably figuring he'd have to jingle in the horses by himself in the morning. I began to think I should be hitting the sack myself. And I was starting to yawn a little.

"I probably ought to be going to bed," said Sally. Maybe she'd seen me yawning.

"Me too. I'm gettin' a little tired an' mornin' comes pretty early."

"Walk me to the lodge," said Sally.

I walked her to the lodge, her hand in mine. I was getting used to holding hands with her when we were alone, but was still a little uncomfortable. But I was getting better.

The next morning, I was up early.

Sally showed up early. I didn't notice any appreciable limp as she walked into the barn. I had been concerned that I might have crippled her a little by dancing on her feet the night before.

As we saddled our horses to bring in the saddle horses, Pat said, "Those boys can sure play good can't they? Now you know why Bud hired 'em."

"Yeah," I said. "But Dave hasn't showed up to help gather the horses. He's been pretty regular about it."

"I thought they were simply wonderful," said Sally. "But what really surprised me was the way you danced!"

Pat assumed a mock look of surprise. "Do you know how to dance, Honey? I guess so, I saw you out there."

"You 'bout danced my feet off, Sally," I said, ignoring Pat's comment. "I was plumb tired out when I hit the sack last night. What time did the boys make it in? I never heard 'em."

"I don't know," replied Pat. "It was pretty late last night or fairly early this morning."

After we gathered the horses and while walking up to the lodge for breakfast, holding hands, Sally asked me, "Honey, what are you going to do with your donkey?"

"You mean Matilda? I don't have any plans for her."

"I thought," said Sally, "if you didn't mind, we could take her and …"

"An' use her for bear bait?" I interrupted.

"No!" Sally was quite adamant about it, although I was only kidding. "I thought we could saddle her with one of the kid's saddles and use her to lead the youngsters around that are too small to ride their own horse. We have two families coming with some smaller children, and she'd be perfect for them. And she's kind of cute."

I felt some twinges of jealousy at Sally's last remark. *Don't be getting' jealous of your own donkey,* I thought.

"Sure," I said. "It's 'bout time she started earnin' her keep. But I really don't want anything to do with leadin' kids around with Matilda."

"You don't have to, silly. The parents lead Matilda with their kids on her."

"That will be fine," I said.

Matilda was soon pressed into duty as a leader donkey. She made a big hit with both the parents and the kids and had her picture taken many times. It wasn't too rough on her, she only did it three days a week and it was good to see her doing something productive.

The Routine is Broken

The summer went on. There was a square dance every week, a branding every other week, and a lot of horseback riding for the dudes every day. Sally, Pat, Dave, and I gathered the horses every morning. Dave's riding skills were getting better, and he was actually becoming some help. Jeff was content to sleep in a little longer each day and just help saddle the horses. He stayed up quite late every night with Linda.

I was pleased to see Jeff and Linda getting together. It gave the hired help and the dudes something else to talk about, besides Sally and me.

Dave hadn't hooked up with any of the other girls and I thought it was because Jim, working with Marie and Josie, was keeping them busy.

Jim had pretty well taken over the head housekeeping duties, leaving Sally more time to help with the horse and cattle work. I even began to appreciate Jim. I really liked the fact that Sally and I were spending more time together, even though it was working. But it was horseback time together.

Bud had gotten the cast off his foot and was getting horseback more often to help. He would ride his big paint horse and Sally would generally ride her grulla gelding. The summer was passing nicely, although much too quickly, I thought.

My colts were coming along nicely and I was riding them with the dude rides on a regular basis. Sally's grulla colt was progressing, although the colt had a little different outlook on things. Sally was doing a nice job of teaching him, although he appeared to be a slow learner and wasn't quite as willing as the other colts. He had somewhat of an attitude problem.

Sally was concerned. "Do you think my colt's a slow learner?"

"No, not really," replied Pat. "Sometimes these slow learners learn things better. They don't seem to forget as fast. Remember, your colt is still a baby an' it takes time."

Sally seemed content with Pat's answer, but was becoming a little frustrated with having to constantly repeat lessons with her colt. I think she was a little jealous of the progress I was making with my colts.

I tried to console her. "A horse learns by repetition," I said. "Doin' the same thing, the same way, over an' over, is the way they learn. It takes a long time."

I also tried to tease her, "Although he might be a little re-tarded," I added.

Sally shot me a dirty look and I immediately wished I had kept my mouth shut.

Missus Abercrombie went riding every day, even though her horse tripped once and she fell off. She wasn't hurt. The horse went all the way down, but luckily, Missus Abercrombie rolled clear.

Sally was close to her when she fell and was immediately off her horse and attending to the older lady. She bailed off her horse and was at Missus Abercrombie's side before I even saw what happened. All I could do was catch her horse. I was too far away to be of any help. Bud caught Sally's grulla and led the horse to where Sally and Missus Abercrombie were standing.

"Are you all right, Virginia?" Bud was obviously concerned.

"Just a little dirty," she replied. She was always aware of her appearance. "It takes more than falling off a horse to injure this old battle ax. Is my horse all right? Where's my camera?"

She was definitely more concerned with her horse's welfare than her own.

"Do you want me to brush you off?" Bud had a mischievous look on his face as he said that.

"No," said Missus Abercrombie, very adamantly, but with an equally mischievous look on her face.

I wondered if there was something going on between them, but quickly dropped the thought. It wasn't any of my business.

We assured her that her horse was all right and she got back on. Bud rode close to her on the way back and I could hear them talking.

Bud asked her, "How many years have you been riding that old horse?"

"After my first year here, when you had me riding anything you wanted, I ..."

Bud interrupted, "I was trying to find a horse suitable for you."

"As I was saying," continued Missus Abercrombie, "I started riding Clover my second year. He's been the only horse I've ridden since then. That's been fourteen or fifteen years."

Bud did some thinking. "That would make him in his late twenties. I think it's time we retired him and found another horse for you to ride. He's done a good job and has earned a rest."

"Do you mean you're going to send him to slaughter?"

"No," said Bud, grinning. "We'll keep him with the saddle horses, we just won't use him. He'll be in the corral every morning and you can visit with him there, if you want. What horse do you want to ride in the future?"

"I really think that gray horse Sally has been riding is cute," answered Missus Abercrombie.

"That's Sally's personal horse and he might be a handful for you," said Bud. "That horse has an attitude. Something else would be a better choice. How about Drygulch that Honey's been riding? He's gentle and Honey has been pretty busy riding those colts."

I bristled at the term "Honey"—an obvious reference to me, but I was getting used to it. I was even introduced to the arriving guests as "Honey," although I could feel my face become flushed every time I heard it.

"Drygulch is an ugly horse," said Missus Abercrombie. "We can select something more suitable at the corrals."

Their conversation regarding a new horse was concluded, ably so by Missus Abercrombie.

Bud slipped away from Missus Abercrombie and joined Sally and me.

"We have some special folks coming next week," said Bud. "They're only staying for three days, but it seems you're acquainted with them, and they specifically asked that you be here. You don't have any other plans to leave, do you?"

"No," I said. I really didn't want to leave with Sally there. "Who are they?"

"You'll know them when you see them."

I tried to remember the guests I had met last year when I'd helped out for a week or so, but couldn't come up with anyone that I thought I had impressed enough to specifically ask for me.

I was puzzled, but set the matter aside because Bud had ridden off to visit with other guests, and it appeared he didn't want to discuss it.

Presently, I forgot all about it, paying attention to my duties with the guests, the colts, and Sally. I helped select a new horse for Missus Abercrombie when we reached the corrals, although she had to look at almost every horse in the corral. She finally picked a horse called Butterscotch, a dun and white gelding.

"I think he will do nicely," she said.

The week passed and one afternoon the following week, I saw a strangely familiar-looking truck pulling into the ranch. I didn't think much of it; Sally and I were busy with other things, namely Sally's colt and the four colts I had been riding. All the colts were progressing nicely; even Beauty was becoming more trustworthy.

"I better go up and greet our new guests," said Sally, when I drew her attention to the approaching pickup.

"I'll go with you," I said. "I'm supposed to know these folks, although I really can't place 'em."

Sally slipped her hand into mine and we started toward the lodge. As we got closer to the new arrivals, I recognized them and tried to slip my hand out of Sally's. She wouldn't let go. I was becoming a little nervous.

As the man took the suitcases out of the back of the truck, he turned around, saw me, put the suitcases down, extended his hand and said, "Hello son!"

Mother turned around, said "Son," and gave me a hug. I was totally embarrassed in front of Sally.

"I'm Sally," she said, letting go of my hand and extending hers toward my dad. "It appears you already know Honey, our wrangler."

"Yes," said my dad, "although we haven't called him 'Honey' since he started school."

My mother had a sly grin on her face. Mother gave Sally a hug and said, "We really haven't heard much about you. I'm anxious to get acquainted."

"This is my brother Tommy an' my sister Betty," I said. I didn't think I wanted my mother and Sally discussing me in front of me.

Bud came out and I made introductions around.

"Help take their things to their rooms, Honey. Your dad and I will get reacquainted."

I picked up two of the suitcases, Sally grabbed one and Tommy got another one, and we went inside.

"I'll take mine in, Honey," said Tommy, grinning wildly. I gave him as dirty a look as I could muster without Sally seeing. After putting the suitcases in the rooms, we rejoined the family and Bud.

They stopped talking when we approached, and I assumed they had been talking about me. I immediately felt selfconscious and ill at ease. The talk turned to the cattle business and the dude business.

"Tomorrow," said Bud, looking at my dad, "We'll gather some cows and have a branding. I understand we have some pretty good cowboys to help us. We'll all have some fun. I'll have the cook show up and we'll have a barbeque."

"Sounds good to me," said my dad. "Are you getting any work out of that boy of mine?"

"Yes," answered Bud.

"That's good! He hasn't done anything for me all summer," replied my dad. They all laughed.

"I'll go down an' turn the horses loose," I said. I was still uncomfortable.

"I'll go with you," said Sally, grabbing my hand.

As we walked down to the barn, I kept trying to look back at my mother and dad to see if they were watching Sally and me.

"You're not very good in social situations, are you?" Sally was curious. "Even with your parents," she added.

"No, I guess not," I said. "Maybe I didn't do so good in social studies with the social graces." I really didn't want to talk about it much. It was a complete surprise to me, my parents showing up. I had been totally unprepared. Why did they come? Were they spying on me? Or did they have other intentions? Did they come to take me home? Was Bud firing me? I didn't have a clue as to what was happening.

"Let's turn these horses loose," I said. "Then it should be about time for supper."

Sally turned her horse loose, and after some extra brushing and kind words, she helped me grain the colts and turn them loose.

Before we started for the lodge, Sally gave me a kiss and said, "You'll be all right, Honey. Don't worry about it."

I guess it was obvious I was concerned.

"How did you know I was a little concerned?"

"You always get a couple of wrinkles in your forehead when you're thinking. They run horizontal. If it's really serious, there's a couple of wrinkles that run vertically, right above your eyebrows."

I was unaware that Sally had paid such close attention as she observed me. I was going to have to watch my body language a lot more closely.

I didn't have much to say at supper. My folks were introduced to the other guests and they were introduced as "Honey's parents." I cringed every time I heard it and I saw my folks grinning as I blushed. They were enjoying the situation.

After an extremely embarrassing supper in which all the talk seemed to be about me, I was ready to head for the bunkhouse. Sally grabbed my hand and we went to the barn to practice kissing. Our lessons had become a regular routine every night.

"What's on your mind?" Sally seemed genuinely concerned.

"I don't know why my folks showed up," I said. "It could be for a variety of reasons an' maybe some of them not good."

"It's very simple," said Sally. "My dad invited them."

"Why?"

"We had some extra rooms available this week and your dad knows my dad. My dad thought it might be kinda nice to have your folks come and see what you do. You're very good at it and Dad's really quite proud of you. You've fit in very well and you're doing a good job of everything, from the guests to the colts you're breaking. Dad is not even charging your folks, it's on him. I'm very pleased also," she added. "I've enjoyed talking with your mother and Betty—they've told me a lot about you that I had only guessed at."

I was becoming very concerned at just what my mother and Betty had told her.

I walked her to the lodge when we were done and went to the bunkhouse. I thought I'd put Tommy on Roman, my mother on Drygulch, and I'd pick something for my dad to ride. Betty would get one of the kid's horses. Sally rode her horse, Beauty, and I rode the bay colt I was breaking.

The next morning, we got everyone mounted and started to gather cattle. As we rode out, I gave my dad and Tommy a general idea of the lay of the land. I thought Mother and Betty would ride with the rest of the dudes, but was surprised when they joined Sally, Dad, Tommy, and me on the longer circle. This was one of the few times when Sally didn't ride next to me and talk with me. She was next to my mother and they were having a lively discussion, frequented with bits of laughter.

I was very interested in what they were talking about and could only catch parts of their conversation. Dad kept me fairly busy by talking about the cattle and the lay of the country. We spread out and started pushing cows and calves toward where we were to meet Bud and the guests.

When we met up with the others and corralled the cattle, Bud told my dad and Sally, "You two get your ropes down; you'll rope for a while. When you get about half of them done, Honey's little brother and I will finish them up."

Dad was riding a dude saddle and didn't have a rope, so I took mine off my saddle and gave it to him with the comment, "Remember, Dad, that's a catch rope! Don't let it get in the habit of missin'!"

Dad laughed and said, "I'll try to remember."

Pat and I did the groundwork and Bud took care of the irons, keeping the fire hot. He also entertained the dudes. As I watched Bud hobble around, I wondered if he'd have a limp due to his busted foot for the rest of his life.

I always liked to watch my dad rope. He made it look so easy and was always in rhythm with the horse and the calf. When he dallied, he didn't even look down at the horn, he just dallied. He missed the first couple of dallies because he wasn't used to the saddle he was riding, but he just spurred his horse up and dallied again. He'd ridden his old saddle for so long, he knew where the horn was, how high it was, and how big around it was. He didn't need to look on his own saddle. But he needed to look on this saddle and when he saw what changes he'd have to make, he made those changes and never looked again. He didn't miss one calf he threw at and I was quite proud of him. He was a good cowboy.

Sally had a good day roping; she didn't miss a calf either. She was using Bud's big paint horse, as her grulla horse wasn't quite ready to start roping off of.

When we had about half the calves branded, Bud called the ropers in. "It's time we ate. The cook's ready, the grub's ready, and I'm hungry."

After the noon meal, Tommy and Bud did the roping. I lent Tommy my rope with the same admonishment I had given my dad.

Tommy missed a couple of calves during his spell at roping, but it was plain he was enjoying himself. "I don't think he's roped anything since we did our brandin' last spring," I said.

"He's pretty good," said Sally. "And your dad is something else! He didn't miss one. I might not be the best roper here today."

Bud missed a few calves and blamed it on his broken foot, which he couldn't place all of his weight on yet. It was a good excuse and nobody challenged him about it.

Sally did make the comment, mischievously, "Maybe you shouldn't rope until you're completely healed."

I think that comment upset Bud a little, because he went out and promptly missed another one. "Maybe you're right, daughter," he said. But he was grinning.

When we finished the branding, we trailed the cows and calves to a pasture where we could gather them easily the next morning and trail them to the summer pasture.

With the day's work done, we rode to the lodge and had supper. After supper, Jeff, Dave, and Jim set up their instruments and we had a square dance.

I was dancing a two-step with my mother. "So this is why you wanted to learn how to dance,"Mom said.

"Yes," I said. "I thought it might come in handy with the dude … er that is, guests."

"And Sally also, I presume. Has she rested her head on your shoulder?"

"Yes."

"Did she fall asleep and fall down?"

"No. I had a good hold on her."

It was hard to put something over on my mom. She was enjoying this little reference to Tommy's comment last winter when Mom was teaching me to dance.

The next day we moved the cattle from the holding pasture to the summer range. Dad and Bud spent a lot of time together, Mother and Sally spent a lot of time together, and I spent a lot of time visiting with the other guests. I was really interested in what Mother and Sally were talking about, but couldn't get close enough to eavesdrop.

When we returned to the ranch, my family made preparations to leave.

I heard Bud invite my folks to stay a little longer, but my dad declined, saying, "We've got plenty to do at home."

He added, "We'll look for you sometime in early October. Plan on staying a couple of days; our accommodations aren't as fancy as yours, but you're welcome to make yourselves at home."

Apparently, Bud was coming out to visit in October, but I couldn't figure out why.

I helped load the suitcases in the back of the pickup. I saw my mother give Sally a big hug and heard her say something about writing on a regular basis. Sally hugged my dad, I shook hands with him, hugged my mother, said so long to Betty and Tommy, and they were off. I felt relieved that they were gone, although I was a little sorry to see them go.

Later that evening, as Sally and I walked down to the barn to resume our kissing practice, I asked her, "What did you an' my mom spend so much time talkin' about the last couple of days?"

"Nothing much," was her reply, "mostly you."

"So," I said, "now I'm 'nothing much,' huh?"

"No," said Sally, laughing, "I didn't mean it that way."

"Then how did you mean it, an' what did my mom say?"

"You're mother told me how she was concerned about you being mostly a loner, not having many friends in school and not mixing with people well. She told me that she thought working out here with the dudes was good for you."

Mom was right about not mixing well with strangers and she was right about this being good for me. I was meeting the new guests better, although I was still a little uncomfortable around strangers.

"So what she said was that I was getting better at the social graces, huh?"

"In a lot more words than that," answered Sally.

I walked Sally back to the lodge, hand in hand, when we had finished our practice. On the way back, we passed Linda and Jeff headed toward the barn.

"I guess Jeff needs a little practice kissin'," I said.

"Oh no," said Sally, "Linda said he's already quite good!"

That came as a surprise to me. I hadn't been aware of what had been happening with the rest of the hired help during the summer.

"Who has Dave hooked up with, Marie or Josie?"

"I think Marie," replied Sally. "Josie and Jim have been spending a lot of time together. But I'm not sure."

"I'll find out when I take 'em ridin' on their next day off. I've noticed that Jim an' Josie have been ridin' together quite a bit." I'd been taking the hired help out for a few horseback rides on their days off, even though Jim and Josie didn't always join us.

A Near Disaster

The summer wore on, although it was passing faster than I wanted it to. My colts were coming along nicely, although the red dun horse was beginning to resist a little. I thought maybe I had been using him a little too much and decided to give him some time off.

Sally's grulla colt, Beauty, was coming along. She'd been riding the colt every day and had just started to take the colt out alone.

One afternoon, the grulla came home alone. I had Roman saddled in the corral and immediately started out to find Sally.

Pat finished saddling a fresh horse and joined me about ten minutes later. We only had a general idea of where Sally had gone. We got out about a mile from the ranch, and Pat said, "You check east, over that ridge an' I'll go west. I hope she ain't hurt. Let out a big holler if you find her an' I'll do the same."

I headed east, topped the ridge, and presently saw Sally, slowly walking up the hill. I trotted down to her.

"You all right?" I was genuinely concerned.

"Yes." Her reply was simple.

"What happened?"

"I was riding along, just enjoying the day, when a sage hen flew up. Beauty spooked and I fell off. I'm really embarrassed."

"Are you sure you didn't get bucked off?" I was teasing Sally a little; everyone has fallen off a horse when it spooked unexpectedly.

"Of course he didn't buck me off," said Sally. She acted like I was insulting her. "I'm a better rider than that!"

I let out a holler to let Pat know that I'd found Sally.

"Well," I said, "climb up here behind me. Roman will ride double. I'll give you a lift home."

I kicked my foot out of the stirrup so Sally could get on. She swung up effortlessly and settled behind my saddle on Roman's back.

"Hold on tight," I said.

"You don't have to tell me that," she replied, as she put her arms around my waist.

Presently, Pat joined us.

"I see you found her," he said.

"Yep, an' I'm takin' good care of her!"

"You bet he is," said Sally, as she squeezed me a little tighter.

"I can see that," said Pat. "You all right, girl? What happened?"

Sally related her experience and added, "I hope you won't tell Daddy."

"He'll probably already know. I left your horse in the corral, still saddled, when I left."

We arrived at the ranch and everyone was concerned as to Sally's welfare.

"You hurt, girl?" Bud was concerned, but not overly so. Bud

knew that if a person rode a lot, they were bound to hit the ground occasionally.

The guests had gathered at the barn and were full of questions regarding what had taken place. One lady kept asking, "Where did you land?"

After being asked the same question so many times, Sally finally answered, "On the ground!" I thought Sally was becoming a little perturbed with the woman, and I was somewhat surprised. I'd never seen her lose her patience with any of the guests or hired help.

The answer, typical cowboy, brought a laugh from everyone and put an end to the questions. Sally excused herself and went to the lodge to change her shirt. She had a lot of dust on it and some on her face to boot.

"If she'd have had a hackamore with a mecate, she could have held on to the horse and you wouldn't have had to go after her. It would have saved her a lot of embarrassment. She's actually quite proud of her cowboy skills. Guess I'll have to get her one," said Bud.

"Her cowboy skills are sure good enough, but don't get her a hackamore," I said. "I figured I'd get her one for Christmas. It would be easy for me, an' save me some problems." I was remembering the shirt I bought by mistake and sent to Sally as a gift last Christmas. "But don't tell her," I added.

"Good enough," said Bud. "Maybe you or Pat ought to go out with her every time she takes the grulla out. I still don't trust that colt a hundred percent."

I volunteered to ride with Sally every day, if the other work permitted it. And I was glad to hear that Bud shared my opinion about the grulla; I didn't think he was entirely trustworthy. But he was a good looking horse and well built.

A few days later we were gathering cattle again to hold another branding. We had a few bulls in the herd and one of them was a little lame. I didn't know if he had foot rot or had got hurt fighting another bull for the right to breed a cow. We put all the cattle, including the lame bull, in the corral.

"Pat, you and Honey get a rope on that bull. We'll stretch him out and see why he's lame. I expect he's been hurt fighting so be careful, he's on the prod. I'll get the guests out of the way."

I got a rope on the bull's horns and Pat missed his shot at the heels. I was glad I was riding Drygulch; he was stout enough to hold the bull. I wasn't sure Roman could do the job. I just had to keep the rope and the bull relatively still while Pat made another loop.

The bull was on the fight and didn't take kindly to our trying to help him out. Drygulch was doing a good job of holding him—he wasn't letting the bull drag us around the corral, but he was moving around quite a bit among the cows. Then, all of the sudden, my rope went slack. I thought for a fraction of a second that my rope had busted. But that was not the case.

The bull had given up fighting the rope and was charging Drygulch and me!

I heard some of the folks hollering, "Look out! Look out!"

I spurred Drygulch to the side and took the slack out of my rope. I managed to let the bull get past us, and then flipped the rope over on the right side of the bull. I didn't think I could flip him like they did in the steer roping contests at the rodeos, but I thought I could slow him down and give Pat a chance to rope his heels.

As I reined Drygulch to the left, figuring on putting on the brakes of the bull, Sally, riding Beauty, came in to rope the heels.

Even though the grulla wasn't ready to be roped off of, Sally was trying to help.

"Get out of there! You'll get hurt," yelled Bud.

But it was too late. The bull hit the end of my rope and it just slowed him down a little. I spurred Drygulch to go faster and take more of the slack out of my rope. But it wasn't fast enough.

The bull was just slowed down a little and immediately took after Beauty. He managed to get his head in Beauty's flanks, and upend Beauty before I could drag him away. I saw Beauty and Sally being flipped over. I didn't have a chance to see how it turned out; I was busy trying to drag the bull away.

The rope had gone slack again and the bull was charging me once more. I gathered up the slack in my rope and dallied up.

Pat had gotten a loop built and came in and roped both heels. We stretched the bull out and he was held down. I looked over quickly to see how Sally was and couldn't see anything. She was on the ground and Bud was bent over her. Missus Abercrombie had gotten in the corral and was kneeling over Sally.

I wanted to go over and see how Sally was, but I knew I'd better stay on Drygulch just in case the bull wanted to cause some more trouble.

Presently, Sally got up with the help of Bud and Missus Abercrombie. I thought she was probably all right. I had been taught that if livestock could get up, they would probably be all right. I thought the same was true of people.

Missus Abercrombie helped Sally out of the corral and Bud walked over to the bull and gave him a swift kick along side the head. "You'll be hamburger for our guests by the end of the week!"

Bud couldn't find any foot rot on the bull, and we assumed he had got hurt fighting another bull. Bud decided not to give him a shot of penicillin; he was going to be slaughtered for the dudes' consumption.

"You want to hurt my daughter, my horses, and my hired help! I'll fix you so you can't hurt anything else." He had a few other choice words for the bull.

"Dave, you go back to the ranch and bring the truck. We're going to take this guy to town soon as we're done here! He'll be hamburger by next week!" Bud was clearly upset.

Dave left and we slipped another rope around the bull's horns. We let the bull up and he kicked off the rope on his heels. I took the lead and Pat followed using the second rope as brakes in case the bull decided to take me again and we took the bull to a separate corral and tied him with both ropes to wait until Dave got back with the truck.

After we had the bull tied up, Sally was in the corral checking over her horse. He had a nasty cut along his flank, but it was superficial, and would heal in time with a little doctoring, although it might leave a scar.

The branding was a very sober affair that late morning. I did most of the roping and Pat and Jeff did the groundwork. Bud did some roping, but Sally didn't do any roping. It was the first time we had held a branding when she didn't rope. But she did do the vaccinating. She walked very tenderly.

Busy with heeling the calves, I didn't have much of an opportunity to talk with her about how she felt. I did manage to ask her, "Are you okay?"

"I'm all right," she answered.

"No she ain't," interjected Bud. "She might have some broken ribs, maybe cracked or at best maybe badly bruised. She's plumb foolish, being in there in that situation. She had no business in there."

"I was just trying to help," she said meekly.

"I don't know what I could have done different," I said.

"Nothing," said Bud. "It's just one of those things. Always expect the unexpected when you're working livestock, especially these old range bulls. They're not used to being handled like show stock!"

I could tell Sally wasn't used to falling out of favor with her father.

Dave showed up with the two-ton stock truck right before we finished. We branded the last calf and made ready to load the bull in the truck. After a couple of tries, Dave got the truck properly aligned to the loading chute.

We tied Bud's rope to mine and took the rope up the chute through the panels on the truck. I didn't have much room, but dallied up. Pat took his rope and was ready to act as brakes in case the bull decided to get in the truck and keep going. I dragged a very reluctant bull onto the truck.

Bud took my rope and tied the bull to the rack in the truck and then untied his rope from mine.

Trying to be humorous, I said, "You'll owe me a new rope to replace that one with all the kinks it'll have in it when you get back! Don't forget to bring it back!"

Bud didn't laugh, just said "Yeah," and turned to Sally. I was wishing I hadn't said anything.

"Get in the truck, daughter," said Bud. "We'll have to have the doc check you over."

"If you're taking her to town, I'm going too!" Missus Abercrombie was not shy about voicing her opinion. "You won't be pleasant company for her being in the mood you're in."

"It's not necessary, Virginia."

"Oh yes it is," replied Missus Abercrombie. "I've got it figured out. Dave here can ride my horse, and Honey and Pat can lead your two back. Now don't argue with me, we're wasting time and this poor girl's welfare is at stake."

"I don't need to go to the doc's," said Sally.

"Yes you do," said Bud. "And Virginia's right, as she usually is," he muttered. He seemed to begrudge Missus Abercrombie her points. He helped Sally and Missus Abercrombie into the truck. "You fellas know what to do with the cattle," he said as he got into the truck.

"Don't wait up for us," was his final comment as he started the truck and headed out.

We got the dudes mounted and started the cattle for the holding pasture. We turned the cattle loose and went back to the corral to get Bud's and Sally's horses. I led the grulla colt back and Pat led Bud's big paint.

Pat had been strangely quiet since the incident. On the way back to the ranch, he said, "I guess it's my fault. If I hadn't missed my first throw at the heels, everything would have been okay."

"No," I said. "Sally shouldn't have been in the corral with that bull on the prod like he was. If I'd have been able to keep my rope tight an' stay out of his way, it would have been better."

"Sally just has to be involved in just about everything that goes on around here," said Pat.

"That's why she's such a good hand," I said.

The rest of the ride home was made in silence. When we got to the barn, we helped the dudes off their horses, unsaddled them, and turned them out in the corral. Pat unsaddled Bud's horse and I unsaddled Sally's. We unsaddled our own horses and turned everything, except a couple of jingle horses, loose.

I kept the grulla colt in and put some salve on his cut. I thought it would be a good idea to keep him in so as I could clean it and doctor it in the morning.

Supper was a solemn affair that night, with a lot of small talk that didn't amount to much. The cook was told what happened and even though Bud had told us not to wait up for them, the cook, Pat, and myself waited for them to return.

When they did finally show up, it was a little late into the night. As they walked through the door, the cook said, "I'll rustle you up something to eat."

"Don't bother," said Bud. "We ate in town."

"How is she?" Pat had asked before I could.

"She's all right," said Bud. "Just some badly bruised ribs. According to the X-rays, there's nothing busted or cracked. She'll need to take it easy for a few days."

Sally had slipped over beside me and slid her hand into mine. "It's no big deal," she said, trying to reassure me. "How's my horse?"

"I put some salve on his cut," I said, "and I kept him in so I could doctor him in the mornin'."

"I'll doctor him in the morning," she said.

"No you won't," said Bud. "Now it's off to bed for everybody! We still have a ranch to run in the morning and it's past my bedtime now! Oh, here's your rope and here's a new one Sally made me get you."

I took the ropes and said, "This ain't necessary."

"Take it!" Bud had put an end to further conversation with his blunt reply.

Missus Abercrombie said, "I sure hope you all like hamburger. That bull will make a lot. Probably feed you guys all summer and most of the winter. I think I'll enjoy eating him myself."

Missus Abercrombie was the only one that wasn't making a big deal out of the situation. She simply accepted the fact that Sally had gotten hurt and she was going to be all right. There wasn't much more that could be done other than a few little courtesies for Sally.

Sally gave me a kiss goodnight, right there in front of everybody and Missus Abercrombie helped her to her room. I was not as embarrassed as I had been at the beginning of the summer.

"It's my fault that it happened," said Pat. "If I hadn't missed ..."

Bud cut him off. "No," he said. "Virginia gave me quite a tongue lashing on the way to the doc's. I've been raising her like a tomboy, letting her do about anything she wanted to on the ranch. It's nobody's fault, if it ain't mine, it's just one of those things.

"I really think Sally enjoyed listening to Virginia chew me out! But, like she says, it's probably too late to do anything about it!"

We left to go to bed and it occurred to me that Sally and I hadn't had our kissing practice. Under the circumstances, I could understand why, but I resolved to tease Sally about it when she felt better.

The next morning, everyone was moving a little slow, having stayed up so late the night before. Sally came down to the corrals but she didn't come out to help us gather the saddle horses.

"Dad and the doc say I can't ride for a few days and my side does hurt a little," she said. "But I'll be watching just the same. I'll doctor Beauty while you're gone."

"I'll do that," I said, as we left to gather the horses. But I halfway suspected that Sally would ignore me.

We resumed the regular ranch routine, with Sally absent for

a few days. When she did start to help out, Bud, Pat, and I cautioned her to slow down and take it easy. But it was not Sally's way to only do things a little bit. She threw herself into everything a hundred percent.

One day after supper, Sally and I went for a ride. "I want to take you to a special place," she said as she led out. We rode out behind the lodge on a faint trail that wasn't used much.

"Where we goin'?"

"I just want to show you something," said Sally.

We rode at a walk for about fifteen minutes until we topped a small rise. The sight below us was of a small valley, circled with pine trees. In the center of the valley was a small area fenced off with steel grated fence. Inside were a number of headstones. It was the Wilson family graveyard. We rode down to the enclosure.

"What are you doin' bringin' me to a graveyard? It's almost dark," I said, trying to be funny.

Sally laughed. "You're not scared are you? This is where my mother is buried," she said. "And Daddy's parents are buried here, too. I don't remember them and only remember my mother a little bit. There are some close friends of the family buried here also, a few hired hands that died while they were working here. This is where Daddy says he wants to be buried when he dies, and this is where I want to be buried. I want to spend the rest of my life on this ranch and be buried here when I die."

"You're not figurin' on dyin' soon are you?" I was still trying to be funny but Sally was very serious.

"I really love this ranch," she said. "I don't think there's a prettier place in the world."

I made no comment, but thought Sally had allowed me to enter one of her special places, reserved for the family only.

When we got back to the ranch, we resumed our kissing

practice. I asked her, "How do you expect me to get better at this if we don't continue to practice? I've missed a couple of days an' bein' a slow learner like I am, we might have to start all over again."

"You're doing all right, Honey," she said, and kissed me again. I was sorta unprepared and it was like we were starting all over again.

A few days later, a familiar looking man came riding into the yard. I'd seen him before, but couldn't quite place where. I thought it might be one of the guys that had stolen my horse and burro the year before, but upon a closer look, it wasn't. The guy tied his horse at the hitch rail and, as he walked into the lodge, he took off his hat.

He was totally bald, his white bald head making a striking contrast to his deeply tanned face. I recognized the sheepherder from the previous summer. It was Bud's brother.

I walked up to the house to say hello and the sheep man and Bud were already talking. Not wanting to interrupt, I started to leave when Bud said, "Hold on there, Honey, I might need you."

"You call him Honey?" There was an amused look on the sheep man's face.

"It's just a nickname," said Bud. "My brother Rod here, you met him last summer, needs a couple of horses. His horses are just about done in and his sheepherders really don't ride good. Can you spare him a couple of your colts?"

It occurred to me that I hadn't heard the sheep man's name until today and I had helped him for a day or two last summer.

"The bay is almost foolproof, the two line-backed buckskins are coming along good an' the red dun is a little reluctant at times. Any one of them should be all right." I really didn't like the idea of giving up any of the colts.

"I'll take the red dun if he's fighting you a little and anyone of the others will be all right."

"They won't take a lot of hard ridin'," I said. "They're only two year olds, still kinda babies. But they do show some good promise."

"That's fine," said the sheep man. "I'll bring 'em back before spring an' they'll be good horses."

"They've been started real well, I'm really pleased with what Honey here has done with them," said Bud.

I was pleased to know that Bud appreciated my efforts with the colts. I had spent a lot of time with them and was proud of the way they were coming along.

"I ran into Fred a few days ago an' he said Sally had got into a wreck. Is she all right? She's the only niece I got, an' I think quite a bit of her."

Fred was the other forest ranger brother. I remember poaching a deer with Rod last summer and the ranger showing up shortly afterward and eating with us. I thought we were going to be arrested until I found out Fred and Rod were brothers.

"Yeah," said Bud. "She's all right. I called Fred from the doc's office and told him to tell you about it. You didn't have to come here to check up on her. But tell her you did, it will make her feel better."

"I feel fine," said Sally. She had been at the door, listening. "And don't you make Uncle Rod lie for me! Hi Uncle Rod!"

She came out and gave her uncle a big hug and a kiss. She was the most kissing person I knew.

"I'll leave you folks to visit," I said. "When do you want the colts ready to go?"

"I'd like to start back now," said Rod.

"Nonsense! You'll stay here tonight and you can leave in the morning," said Bud, "You need a little brush with civilization now and then."

"Fred comes by about once a month to check on me," said Rod. "That's about as much civilization as I need."

"You just stay here tonight and get something good to eat. You might provide some good entertainment for our dudes. You're as close to a mountain man as there is left. Besides that, we've got a lot of catching up to do. Do you know that Honey's dad shot the mountain lion you missed? He'd got a couple of our calves. I'm going over to his place in October to pick out some replacement heifers. Do you want to go and meet the man that got the mountain lion?"

"Really?" Rod looked surprised. "That lion got some of my sheep, too. Looks like we owe your dad a debt of gratitude. I might have to go with you. How'd you come by the tag 'Honey'?"

I was becoming a bit embarrassed. Now I knew what had brought my dad to the ranch earlier in the summer and what he and Bud were discussing. Funny, I thought they were talkin' about me.

"I gave it to him," said Sally. "Doesn't it fit him well?"

"I'd better get back to work," I said, wanting to leave and avoid further embarrassment. "I'm sure Sally an' Bud will delight in tellin' you all about it."

"Oh, we will," said Sally, as I started to leave. She had an impish look on her face as she made the last comment.

I was getting used to the nickname "Honey." I'd been introduced to all the guests all summer as Honey. Even though I was getting used to it, I was still embarrassed by it. The little kids were even calling me Honey.

At supper that night, I was amused by Rod. He kept up a running dialogue for the guests' benefit. I assumed it was because he'd spent so much time alone, taking care of his sheep. But he had a good line of preposterous stories to tell the dudes and they really enjoyed him.

The next morning, Rod was at the corral with his coffee when we ran the saddle horses in. I pointed out the red dun and the two line-backs.

"Either one of them will do," he said.

"They're all gentle an' you can catch 'em anywhere's," I said. "Pat did a good job when he halter broke them. I've done a little roping off them an' dragged some calves to the fire. They still need some work on their neck reinin', but they're coming along fine. They'll be fine ranch geldings an' about any dude will be able to ride 'em."

Bud joined us with his coffee. He was still using his cane occasionally, when his ankle started to hurt him some. "You need to leave your old horse here for a while, Rod. He looks like he could use a rest. I'll lend you a good horse to use until October, and then you can pick up your horse after we come back from Honey's folks. That will give him a good rest and I've got a good gelding you can use. He's a little too much for the dudes and he needs the riding."

"That'll work," said Rod. "If you add a few feet to that cane, you can come out an' help me with the sheep. Looks like you're all set to start—you've already got a sheep hook!"

Bud gave Rod a dirty look, laughed, and had Pat catch a horse he called Flower for Rod. "Don't let his name fool you," said Bud. "He's all horse and almost bucked Pat off this spring the first time he saddled him."

"Flower, huh? Is he a rose or a pansy?"

"He's more like the thorns on a rose," said Pat.

I'd seen Rod ride a bucking horse last summer and was sure

the horse wouldn't give him much trouble. Rod was a good bronc rider.

Rod saddled Flower and the horse did crow hop a little, but not bad.

"If that's as bad as he gets, it won't be bad at all," said Rod.

"It gets worse," said Pat. "Just stay awake on him until you get him rode down a little. He hasn't been used much this summer an' he's kinda snakey."

Rod gave him a knowing look. I handed him the lead rope to the red dun and one of the line-backs. I'd tied the lead to the line-back to the red dun's halter. Rod looked at my work, nodded his head in approval and set off.

"You're coming to our place in October?" I said to Bud.

"Yes, I need some replacement heifers. I'm going to cull pretty heavy this fall. Your dad sold me some good ones a few years ago and I think he'll have some more. Are you going to be there?"

"Of course," I said. "I'll be in school, but I'll be there."

"I'll have Pat and Rod with me. You got room to put us up?"

"Yep," I said. "I'll warn Mother an' have her fix her best supper."

Bud laughed. "That won't be necessary."

Parting Ain't Such Sweet Sorrow

The summer was passing. I hadn't given it much thought until I received a letter from Mother indicating when school started and telling me that I needed to be home early enough to get some new school clothes. And I needed to leave myself adequate travel time.

I got with Bud and we discussed when I needed to leave. We settled on a date that would allow me enough time to ride my horse and lead Matilda home. I only had about two weeks of work left. Then I asked Bud if he wanted me to come back next year.

"Most assuredly, most assuredly! You've done a real fine job with the colts and the dudes! You have a job here anytime you want it!" Bud was very positive about hiring me back next year. "And you can bring your saddle horse and your donkey. That donkey made quite a hit with the guests that had small youngsters. She more than paid her way. And we'll have some of those spotted yearlings for you to start; they'll be two year olds then, although I plan on selling some of them this fall. There'll be plenty for you to do. We'll probably keep you busier than you were this year."

"I was thinkin' I might drive here. I'll have a driver's license next year an' I figure I'll get a truck. I could get here a little earlier. It's only a five or six hour drive from our place to here accordin' to my dad, but it's about a week's horseback ride."

"Well, you do as you see fit, but I would like to have that burro."

"I don't really want to sell her," I said.

"I don't want to buy her," said Bud. "But she would be nice to have around for the guests. She's kind of a conversation piece."

I brought up the subject of leaving with Sally when we went to the barn to practice our kissing.

"I knew this time would come," she said. "When do you have to go?"

"I need to be home in time to get some school clothes. It'll take about a week to ride home leadin' Matilda. I'll only be here a couple more weeks. I talked with your dad, an' he wants me to come back next year an' I told him I would. Is that all right with you?"

"My dear stupid, dumb, loving cowboy, of course! What did you think, Honey?"

With her using the stupid dumb cowboy, I thought we were leaving off where we had been last fall, when I got my first letter from her. But I suspected she was being sarcastic. She assured me she was with a big, passionate kiss.

"I don't know how I'm goin' to get along without you," I said. "I guess," I continued, "I'll have to find someone else to practice kissin' with."

"WHAT?!!" Sally had become obviously upset. "You better not! I don't think you need any more practice and if you get a little rusty during the winter, we'll get you back in shape in the spring!"

"But I've sorta enjoyed the practice sessions," I said. I was enjoying teasing her about this.

"I have too," she said. "But, I'll be very disappointed in you if you feel like you need to practice with someone else. And you don't need any practice dancing either!"

"You mean to say that I'm pretty good?"

"You will need more practice," she said, "but only with me!"

"Well," I said, "if you're goin' to be so narrow minded about it, I guess it will have to be that way."

"What do you mean narrow minded?"

I could tell I was getting to her, and it was fun.

We did our practicing and I walked her to the lodge, hand in hand.

Before she went in, she asked me, "Are you going to leave the same way you did last summer?"

"What do you mean?"

"Last year you just rode off. You didn't even get off your horse to say goodbye. And I had my best dress on!"

"I'll probably leave the same way," I said. "I'm not much at public displays of emotion."

"Still my shy, bashful, backward cowboy," she said. "We might have to work on that a little in the future."

"You mean I still have to work on social graces?"

"Oh yes," she said. "But I promise I'll help you!"

She kissed me good night and went into the lodge and I went to the bunkhouse.

I spent a fitful night that night, thinking about the summer coming to an end. I had really enjoyed the summer and the time I had spent with Sally. I thought I was going to miss this job. The work wasn't hard, just long days, and I was finding it easier to get along with the dudes. I even got to the point where I enjoyed them some. Bud had some good horses to ride and it had been fun riding the colts during the summer. I really wasn't looking forward to leaving. I resolved to work a little harder to keep my mind off leaving. If it meant spending a little more time with the dudes, I resolved to do it. Besides, it might help me with my social graces.

The horseshoer came and he shod Roman for me along with some ranch horses. I trimmed Matilda, her feet were tough and she had made it home without shoes last year. I couldn't see shoeing her, then pulling them off when I got home.

The horseshoer always drew a crowd when he showed up and there wasn't an exception when I trimmed Matilda. I got the job done and had a lot of fun joking with the dudes.

The last two weeks of the summer went too fast. I noticed that Sally was dancing a little closer to me when we did the two-step at the weekly dances. However, she was still active in entertaining the guests and gave a hundred percent when we were out riding, checking the cattle.

Occasionally, we'd find a cow that needed some doctoring and we'd rope her. I'd generally rope the cow's head and Sally would pick up the heels. When I'd miss the head, Sally would come in and rope the cow and I'd pick up the heels. I thought we made a pretty good team, although nobody kept time like they do at the rodeos. I even did some daydreaming about the two of us entering the team roping in some rodeos, and, of course, winning. Roping out in the open, with the sagebrush and the trees and some rocks, is a lot different than it is in a rodeo arena.

The night before I was scheduled to leave, Bud called me

into his office after supper. He had a check for me and some cash money.

"This is some tip money the guests have left for you during the summer," he said as he handed me the cash.

I took it and put it in my pocket without counting it.

"And here's your wages for the summer, and a bonus." He handed me a check.

I took the check, folded it and put it in my pocket.

"You never even counted the money or looked at the check," said Bud. "How come?"

"No sir," I said. "If I didn't trust you, I wouldn't have come to work for you in the first place."

"Doing business kinda like the old timers," said Bud.

"That's what my dad taught me," I said.

Sally knocked and came into the room. She had a package in her hand.

"This is for you," she said, handing me the package.

I was totally dumbfounded. I hadn't expected any gifts, and I didn't have anything to give her. I was embarrassed. Sally took my hand and led me from the room.

As I was leaving, I thanked Bud for the paycheck.

Bud said, "You can get some groceries from the cook. He'll have them ready for you in the morning."

I didn't have a chance to thank him again.

"This isn't much," said Sally. "But I want you to think of me often."

I opened the package. Inside was the hackamore I had lent to her and a photo album. There were a lot of pictures of Sally riding her grulla horse and Bud's horse. There were some pictures of just Sally and there were pictures of me, riding my colts,

Drygulch, and Roman. There were even some pictures of Sally and me.

"Where did you get all theses pictures? I don't remember a lot of cameras around," I said. "You take this; you'll need it to ride the grulla. We'll put him in a snaffle bit next year."

"That's your hackamore, you take it," said Sally.

"Missus Abercrombie took a lot of the pictures, most of them in fact. Some came from the guests. I hope you like them."

"I certainly do. I'll take good care of them. I'll put them in the bunkhouse."

Sally accompanied me to the bunkhouse then we went to the barn to continue our practice sessions.

"It will be a rough day for me tomorrow when you leave," said Sally. "I hope I don't cry. I did last year, you know."

"I didn't know," I said. "But there's nothin' to cry about."

"What do you mean, nothing to cry about? You're leaving, we're emotionally involved and you don't think there's anything to cry about?"

I was surprised to learn we were emotionally involved. It was readily apparent that Sally had given this situation more thought than I had. I didn't know what to do or say. My only thought was that I'd have to improve in my social graces, at least enough so that I could tell what was going on around me.

The next morning I saddled Roman. Pat and I gathered the saddle horses. Dave had been a little lax about helping to gather the horses, most of his spare time was being spent with Marie.

"I understand you'll be leaving this morning," said Pat.

"Yep," I said, but not in high spirits.

"Bud tells me you're coming back next year."

"Yep."

"I'll have them yearlings ready for you. They'll be two year olds an' big enough to start ridin' next spring."

"I hope they're as good as the ones this year. They were good colts. The worst one was Sally's grulla. Where is she this mornin'?"

"Don't know," said Pat.

We found the horses and brought them in on a run. Sally wasn't at the corrals when we got there. I caught Matilda and put her pack saddle on her. I went to the kitchen and got the groceries the cook had for me and took them down to the barn. I got the rest of my gear, took it down to the barn and got Matilda packed. I made sure I packed the photograph album Sally had given me and the new rope Bud had given me. Then I went to the lodge for breakfast.

I still hadn't seen Sally. I didn't know where she was or what she was doing.

After breakfast, I said goodbye to all the guests and shook hands with Bud and Pat.

"I'll come back up to say goodbye again before I leave," I said.

I went to the barn, tightened Roman's cinch, got Matilda's lead rope on and rode to the lodge. All the guests, the hired help, and Bud and Sally were gathered on the porch.

Sally looked like she had been crying and Bud had his arm around her, as if he was giving her moral support.

I waved at the people and started to turn Roman to leave, then stopped. I motioned for Pat to come over. I looped Matilda's lead rope around my saddle horn, got off, and gave the reins to Pat.

"Hold him for a minute, would you?"

I walked up to Sally, put my arms around her and gave her as passionate a kiss as I could. She was a little surprised at my action, but recovered quickly. While I still had my arms around her, she whispered, "I love you!"

I was surprised and didn't know what to say, and after a very awkward moment of silence, all I could say was, "Me too."

I backed away to the sound of all the guests applauding. Some were even whistling. Missus Abercrombie and Bud had big smiles on their faces. I think Bud had been outright laughing.

I backed away another step and on impulse, took off my hat and took a big bow. I could feel my face flush and was anxious to get going. To the sound of more applause and even some cat-calls, I walked to Roman, took my reins from Pat, got on and rode away.

I heard Sally yell, "They'll be a letter waiting for you when you get home!"

A hundred yards away, I turned in the saddle, made one final wave and rode off. I saw Sally waving. She went into the house without Bud's help.

I kinda felt proud of myself. I had taken the initiative and kissed Sally goodbye in front of everyone and although I was red-faced about it, I didn't feel all that uncomfortable about it.

The first day's riding home was uneventful and I soon got used to the routine I had become accustomed to the previous summer. As the days passed, I quickened my pace a little. The promise of a letter from Sally was too inviting to take my time. And I needed to do some shopping for school clothes and buy a hackamore for Sally for Christmas!